Forgotten Specters

The Fated Wings Series Book 2

C.R. Jane

Forgotten Specters by C. R. Jane

Copyright © 2018 by C. R. Jane

Cover by Ever After Cover Design

All rights reserved.

No portion of this book may be reproduced in any form or by any electronic or mechanical means, including information storage and retrieval systems, without written permission from the author, except for the use of brief quotations in a book review, and except as permitted by U.S. copyright law.

For permissions contact:

crjaneauthor@gmail.com

This book is a work of fiction. Names, characters, businesses, places, events, locales, and incidents are either the products of the author's imagination or used in a fictitious manner. Any resemblance to actual persons, living or dead, or actual events is purely coincidental.

Join C.R. Jane's Readers' Group

Stay up to date with C.R. Jane by joining her Facebook readers' group, C.R.'s Fated Realm. Ask questions, get first looks at new books/series, and have fun with other book lovers!

Join C.R.'s Fated Realm

Dedications and Acknowledgments

For Willia.

The Fated Wings Series

First Impressions
- Forgotten Specters
- The Fallen One (a Fated Wings Novella)
- Forbidden Queens
- Frightful Beginnings (a Fated Wings Short Story)
- Faded Realms
- Faithless Dreams
- Fabled Kingdoms
- Forever Hearts

Forgotten Specters

Eva has forgotten something.

Hints of another life, and who she really is, are whispered to her in dreams, visions, and in her interactions with people who seem to know more about her than they let on.

Eva's struggle to find out who or what she is, all while navigating the real world for the first time, is complicated by the confusing relationships she's begun to develop with the three men she's fallen for.

Will Eva ever find her happy ending, or will forgotten specters change the course of all she is coming to know?

"Some of the most beautiful things worth having in your life come wrapped in a crown of thorns."

—— Shannon L. Alder

"The little queen's mother and father had said that she would live on, for a long time, and that her tears would magnify the life around her forever more, but they had not explained how she should go about going on."

—— Meia Geddes, The Little Queen

"Do we not each dream of dreams? Do we not dance on the notes of lost memories? Then are we not each dreamers of tomorrow and yesterday, since dreams play when time is askew? Are we not all adrift in the constant sea of trial and when all is done, do we not all yearn for ships to carry us home?"

—— Nathan Reese Maher

Prologue
Eva

I was striding through the haunting, beautiful landscape again. I looked around for the child that had accompanied me before, but I was completely alone. There was a chill in the air, the balmy breezes from previous visits nowhere to be found. This time when I looked out in the distance, I didn't see just rolling hills covered in lush trees. This time, I saw a sparkling white structure, castle like in its design and enormity, standing tall in the distance. It called to me, feeling more like home than anywhere else I had been. I felt a longing in my heart for it. I could feel it beckoning to me, asking me to return to its depths. I began to walk quickly towards the building, my tentative steps turning to a full run as the castle seemed to get farther and farther away as I tried desperately to approach it.

I stumbled, falling to the ground and scraping my knee, losing sight of the building momentarily. When I stood up, the white building had disappeared, replaced by the ash strewn landscape that always replaced my paradise in the end. I let out a wail of sorrow, knowing intrinsically that I had lost something irreplaceable to my heart, something that I would never be able *to find again. I watched a drop of blood slowly collect in my scrape before it dropped into the grey powder that covered the ground. A flash of light almost blinded me.*

And then I woke up.

One
Eva

My senses came alive as wintergreen and leather enveloped me. A calloused hand swept some of the hair off my face. My eyes slowly opened. Mason's twinkling indigo eyes stared back at me looking concerned. "What happened?" I asked.

"I'm not sure," he replied. "I was about to introduce you to Beckham, and you just fainted," he said worriedly.

I sat up. Mason had moved me off to the side of the room, behind some plants to give me more privacy. Where was Beckham? He had said something, something important, but I couldn't remember what it was.

"Where did Beckham go?" I asked Mason.

"He and Vanessa went to go see if they could find a doctor for you," he replied. "We were all worried about you."

I grimaced. "Can you please text him or something and tell him I'm fine?" I asked in dismay. The last thing I wanted was to ruin the night with being taken to the hospital.

"Are you feeling okay? Should we leave?" Mason asked.

I pushed myself up and stood very ungracefully,

smoothing down my dress and making sure nothing had torn. I looked up at Mason and smiled.

"I'm fine. I promise. I just haven't eaten very much today so my blood sugar is probably low," I told him.

"Well let's go fix that. There's enough stars fucking starving themselves tonight to leave plenty of food for us," he said laughing, the gravelling richness floating over me.

Mason grabbed my hand and led me towards another room where service stations with stacks of every kind of food imaginable were set up all around.

"Did Beckham say anything strange?" I asked, still struggling to grasp what had happened.

"Not that I saw," said Mason. "I don't think he actually had the chance to formally introduce himself since you fainted."

Mason was interrupted by an excited voice calling my name. I turned around and saw Lexi. She was dragging a relaxed looking Lane behind her.

"I'm so glad you're here!" she squealed. "Isn't this just the coolest thing ever? I can't believe it. Selena is going to shit her pants when she finds out we got to go to the Grammy's and she didn't!"

Mason was laughing at Lexi's enthusiasm.

"You and Lane hit it off last night didn't you?" he smirked.

Lexi's enthusiasm seemed to ramp up a notch if that was possible.

"Oh my gosh. Lane is the absolute sweetest!" she squealed louder.

Lane appeared to be out of it at this point, smiling goofily at nothing in particular. Lexi let go of Lane and grabbed my arm.

"Let's get food! Everything looks so amazing!" she cried.

Mason smiled at me indulgently and released my other

arm. "Don't go too far," he laughed. "The show is going to start any minute."

Lexi started piling everything on her plate at once. I was a little more circumspect in my choices as there were a lot of things I hadn't heard of before. I hadn't lied to Mason though, I really hadn't eaten, and I was starving. Maybe I had fainted because of that. I hoped we would see Beckham again. I wanted to see if he said anything when he saw me this time. I wondered if I was losing my mind and imagining things since Mason hasn't seemed to notice anything strange. The feeling that I was forgetting something was heavy on my mind.

Lexi was chattering about the night before. Evidently she had made quite the impression on Lane, having "screwed his brains" out in a bathroom at Covet. I laughed, while also blushing profusely, as she described an older woman walking in and her reaction to seeing Lexi mid-thrust, her bare butt hanging out for all to see. I was laughing at something else Lexi was saying when Mason found me again.

"Are you ready to go in?" he asked.

I swallowed the bite of chocolate tart I had been stuffing in my mouth and nodded, taking his hand when he offered it.

The auditorium was massive and filled to the brim with gorgeous, richly dressed people. Mason led me to the row of seats right in front of the stage, where the rest of the band was waiting. Lexi and Lane had followed us to the row. I sat down, my mouth gaping at the spectacle everywhere. Stars and camera crews were everywhere. Mason turned to me.

"You have to cheer for me when we perform tonight even though you just saw me in concert."

"You're performing tonight?" I asked. He looked at me quizzically.

"Have you never watched the Grammy's before?" he asked. I froze. I had gotten better at hiding how out of touch I was with everything, but this had been a slip-up. I laughed awkwardly.

"Not for awhile," I said. "I must have forgotten how it works." He stared at me for a second, seeming to be able to see right through me, before deciding to let it go.

The show started. I was entranced by all the performances. I had always loved music, and it had been one of the hardest things about living with the Andersons that no music was allowed. I soaked up the symphony of sounds around me. Mason had just left to get ready to perform, kissing me quickly on the lips before he left. My fingers traced my lips, melting inside at such a sweet gesture. The Riot had already won a few awards for "Best Song" and "Record of the Year", from the whispers around me it was expected Mason would win "Artist of the Year" as well. Just then someone slid into Mason's seat, catching me by surprise.

"I'm used to girls fainting at the sight of me, but I have to say that was a first," came a voice that reminded me of chocolate. It was smooth and warm, almost like it was wrapping me up in a big hug. I turned to look at the newcomer. It was Beckham. A sigh involuntarily left me at the sight of him. He was examining me as well, wearing a small grin. Beckham Stone was a heartbreaker if there ever was one.

Supremely gorgeous, more Greek god than anything else, he radiated a golden light from his every pore. Like with Damon and Mason, I immediately felt a rush of belonging, like he was someone that was already mine, and had been for quite some time.

"Well I do try to please," I answered, smiling, pleasantly surprised at how steady my voice came out.

"I don't believe we've actually met," he said. "I'm Beckham...and you are Eva I presume?"

"Yes," I said, my voice squeaking despite my attempts to play it cool. He had just touched my hand and the same tingles

I felt whenever Mason or Damon were near had spread all over me.

"Why in the world are you spending time with such an ugly fellow?" teased Beckham. "You must feel sorry for him or something to be seen with a guy as hard on the eyes as Mase."

Beckham now had a big grin on his face, like the whole world was a joke. I could feel Lexi swooning beside me as she listened in.

"Did you lose your date?" I flirted back. "Or did she find something better?"

"You know, Eva. Your mama must not have taught you manners because it isn't polite to be mean to people you just met," he answered, smiling even bigger now.

Despite his teasing a little tinge of sadness ran through me. I wished I had a "mama" that had taught me those manners. I must have had a look in my face because Beckham's smile faded.

"Hey," he said, lightly touching my hand. "Did I go too far?" I shook my head, determined to get over myself.

"Nope. I was just feeling sorry for myself. Nothing that you did." He tilted his head, about to ask more when Mason's voice sounded up on the stage in front of us. He was looking down at Beckham and I with a troubled look on his face.

"This goes out to Eva," he announced to the crowd suddenly, who went crazy at his pronouncement.

Mason launched into a song I hadn't heard the night before and once again everything was forgotten around me. His voice enveloped me, soaring me to new heights. There was a feeling of magic in the air, like everything you had ever wished for was within reach. The whole auditorium hung on his every word. I had been listening to other bands all night and none of the other singers had made me feel like this. Was it because I was biased towards Mason, or was he really just that amazing of an artist?

The last notes of the song ended, and I found myself letting out a breath I didn't realize I had been holding. I turned to Beckham, wondering what his reaction to Mason's music had been. Beckham had an amused smile on his face. I saw him casually salute Mason and laugh to himself. I looked back at Mason who was grinning down at me. I watched Mason and the rest of the band exit off the stage. Mason had told me they would be doing a few interviews after the performance before he would be able to return to his seat.

I turned my attention back to Beckham who had been looking at me intensely, much to my surprise. I began to play with my hair self-consciously. The once jovial Beckham looked like he had something on his mind. He went to say something, and was interrupted by Mason, who for some reason seemed to have rushed back to his seat instead of doing interviews.

"Everything okay here?" Mason said, noticing the intensity that was rippling between Beckham and me.

"Everything is fine Mase," laughed Beckham, resuming the breezy attitude he had before. "Just getting to know Eva a little bit better," he continued, standing up from Mason's seat so that Mason could replace him. Mason's face gentled as he looked at me.

"She's amazing isn't she?" he said smiling.

"Yes, she is," whispered Beckham, so softly that I wasn't sure Mason heard him. "Well, I better head back to my date," said Beckham. "Let's ride together to the after-parties though Mase," continued Beckham, clapping Mason on the shoulder before departing.

"Sounds good Beck," Mason said distractedly, his attention turning towards the act starting up on stage. Beckham began to walk away, peering back over his shoulder with a look that promised we weren't done yet. A chorus of sighs sounded from woman around me as he walked off, the delicious suit he was wearing showing off his fine form.

I settled back into my seat, my mind musing over my interaction with Beckham. Mason reached out and grasped my hand, his thumb moving up and down to the beat of the song that was starting. I smiled and sighed. These boys were going to be the death of me.

Two
Beckham

There have been a lot of moments in my life. Moments of joy, moments of despair. So many moments. But I knew intrinsically that meeting Eva tonight would go down as the most important moment so far in my long life. It was a struggle to keep my emotions from bleeding out onto my face as we approached Mason and Eva. I doubted either Vanessa or Mason would be comfortable at the way I wanted to throw myself at her feet and beg her to keep me forever.

She looked indescribable, like everything I had ever wanted wrapped in one glowing package. She radiated this light that reflected out into the room, attracting everyone's attention. Her ebony dress clung to a frame that the gods must have been envious over. Perfect curves from head to toe. Her hair hung in gold waves down her back, and her eyes stared intensely back at me, sucking me in with their clear depths. In the instance before she had fainted, when Mason had introduced me, I had seen a look on her face of recognition and possession, like I belonged to her. As I had approached, a strand of thought had strayed across my mind, feeling like an actual memory more than anything else, of the two of us in a different time.

Eva had been dressed in a glimmering cream dress, and I had reached a black gloved hand to stroke her face, calling her "Your Majesty" as I did so.

I was sure I hadn't ever met Eva though, and was confused at where such a thought had come from or why I had been calling her that. As the thought faded from my mind, Eva's eyes had rolled back, and she began to collapse. Mason grabbed her before she hit the ground.

My hands clenched, desperate to hold her. From the possessive way Mason was holding Eva, and the warm look he had been giving her as we approached, I knew my friend was in deep. The only problem was, I felt that I could be in deep with Eva as well. Again, that feeling of awareness rushed over me, whispering to my heart that I had in fact always felt this way about Eva, despite the fact that my brain knew we were just meeting.

Mason had sent me a text telling me Eva was fine while I was looking for a doctor to look at her. Vanessa, upon reading the text over my shoulder, had immediately delightedly dragged me to socialize with various industry people. I was frustrated, I wanted to make sure that Eva was all right in person.

I was distracted as Vanessa chattered with some singer whose name I couldn't remember. Seeing Eva had seemed to open up a sieve inside of me. Flashes of strange scenes kept floating through my memory, feeling so real that I could reach out and touch them. Every single scene featured Eva at its center. In some she was laughing, her head thrown back with delight at something I had said to her. In others we were riding palominos in an open lush field, the wind pulling her streaming gold hair behind her as we raced to some unknown destination. In others we were lying in a lacey, white bed, gauzy curtains cocooning us in a space that was all our own.

My cock involuntarily stirred as I remembered the smooth feel of her skin, the way that her lips tasted as I pressed them to mine, my tongue pushing to enter and lick the sweet taste of her mouth.

"Honey," Vanessa's voice stirred me from what had seemed more like reminiscing than figments of my raging libido's imagination. A taste of sugar and honey lay heavy on my tongue, so real that I felt sorrow that Eva's lips weren't on mine at that moment.

"Sorry, what were you saying," I said hurriedly, staring down with what I hoped looked like interest at Vanessa.

Vanessa and I had been friends since I first decided to try my hand at Hollywood. I had never hooked up with her, despite the longing I saw in her eyes when she looked at me, determined not to use her for something I couldn't follow through with. I had actually, finally been going to tell her we could try and date tonight. I had grown so tired of dating people I couldn't trust and Vanessa had been there for me for years. But that thought had been before I met Eva tonight.

"I was just telling Charise about the new project you are working on," she said sweetly.

"Oh yes, I'm very excited about the opportunity to work on such an amazing story," I answered automatically, ready made responses always on the tip of my tongue since no one bothered to ask me anything interesting. My attention trailed away again as Charise started chattering about a project she had recently worked on, as if I actually cared. I felt anxious. I wanted to go back to Eva and find a way to ask her if what I was seeing was real. If she had the same memories inside of her. I smiled automatically as Vanessa said her goodbyes. She waved once more and then took my arm so that I could escort her into the auditorium to catch our seats before the start of the show.

Three
Eva

Mason could best be described as giddy as the show ended. The Riot had swept the show, winning all of the awards they had been nominated for and breaking the previous record for most Grammy's won in a year. I was swept up in the excitement and Mason's happiness, loving this playful side of him.

The band was eager to get to the after-parties, ready to bask in the praise of the other guests over their success. Mason pulled me to him and kissed me hard before stepping back, grabbing my hand, and pulling me towards the doors. He immediately was inundated by congratulations and admiration as we walked, everyone trying to get a piece of him before we left. Mason encircled me with his arms and I felt deja vu from the previous night when we had been attacked by the swarms of photographers. I stiffened involuntarily at the memory, but Mason didn't seem to notice.

We eventually made our way out to the limo line, Beckham and Vanessa meeting us at the doors to walk out with us. Lexi and Lane had disappeared somewhere else with the rest of the band. Beckham seemed to hover protectively by my side as Mason walked behind me. I liked the feeling of them closing in around me. It made me feel protected from the peering eyes around us. Mason had Vanessa and I enter the limo first, he and Beckham following behind us.

As soon as we sat down, Mason pulled me into a long kiss that made my whole body heat up. The fact that I could feel Beckham's eyes intensely watching us pushed my temperature up even more.

"That was fucking amazing!" said Mason, seeming to be talking about both the show and the kiss.

"Proud of you buddy," said Beckham. I noticed that he kept some distance from Vanessa. I had thought that they were together, but I hadn't seen him act anything more than respectful towards her. She was looking away from Mason and I, staring out the window at the buildings passing by.

"Are we going to Tommy's party?" asked Beckham.

"Ya, I promised him we would stop by for at least an hour," answered Mason, wrapping an arm around me and pulling me close.

I had noticed that Mason never stopped touching me. He was super affectionate, which I loved. This gruff rocker had the sweetest center. Beckham and Mason chatted back and forth while we drove. Occasionally Vanessa would interject a comment. I stayed mostly quiet, content to sit back and listen to the industry gossip. The three of them seemed to know everything about everyone. Vanessa was a publicist evidently, although not Beckham's. I gleaned from the conversation that they had been friends for a long time. Beckham had been quick to stress the word friends, with a look towards me as he did so. Involuntarily I felt butterflies build up in my stomach.

I obviously didn't know any of these men very well, but all three of them made me feel like fireworks were going off inside of me. Damon was so sweet and giving towards me. The gestures he had made for me, both big and small, had made me feel for the first time in my life that I was actually safe and cared for. Daydreaming about what he was like had gotten me through my last few months with the Andersons. To find out that he was ten times more amazing in person than in my dreams had been breathtaking to experience. He had been willing to make the extra effort and go slow with me, when I could tell that was not his usual style. He paid close attention to things that I cared about, and made it a part of our relationship. I loved that about him.

Mason was my gruff teddy bear. He made me feel sexy and wanted. I loved that he always wanted to touch me, and that he was so generous with his affection. He made me feel like I was the center of his world in the very short time I had known him. I wondered if that would continue when he went back on tour.

I knew Beckham least of all, but already I could tell he was like a ray of light. He brought out happiness in those around him. Mason laughed and joked with Beckham more than I had seen him do with anyone else. Although I had just met him, I strangely felt more familiarity with Beckham than I did with Mason or Damon. Beckham felt like coming home. All three felt important, like I had known them forever, but my interactions with Beckham had made my heart ache a bit, like I had been missing him my whole life and just now gotten him back.

"Look out your window, Eva," said Mason, bringing me out of my reverie. "You can see Tommy's house from here, it's quite the spectacle.

I eagerly scooted over to the window to look outside. Everything I had experienced since leaving the Anderson's was so new and sensational, I didn't want to miss a thing.

Tommy's house was a spectacle (whoever Tommy was). It was more than a mansion, it was more like a gigantic glass fortress. It looked like it was made of all glass. It must have had some kind of special glass on it because although you could tell that every light was on in the house, you couldn't see inside. My eyes widened as the limo got closer. I could see the ocean behind the mansion. I itched to skip the party and go walk along the beach. We finally pulled up to the front of the house. Mason got out first, and held out a hand to help me out. I wobbled a bit on my heels, I wasn't used to wearing them. I felt hands on my waist from behind me, helping to steady me. Again, I had images of Mason in front of me, Beckham behind me, both touching me at the same time. I involuntarily shivered.

"Mason," a voice somewhat slurred from in front of me.

An aging rocker, with skin almost like leather that had seen way too much sun, and way too much alcohol (judging by his blood shot eyes), waved to us. It was impossible for me to tell exactly how old he was. His clothes looked like something a young person would wear, skinny black jeans and a silver button up shirt that was deliberately unbuttoned so that a myriad of necklaces could be displayed. He had dark, black, curly hair that was held back with a black bandana. He looked...fun? Mason let go of me to walk over to the guy who I was assuming was Tommy, and clap him on the back in one of those man hugs. Mason laughed at something that Tommy said and gestured me over. I walked over, Beckham had let me go after a light caress to my waist.

"Eva, I want you to meet Tommy," Mason exclaimed, looking delighted that we were meeting.

I immediately liked Tommy. While I could tell he appreciated my looks, he didn't leer at me as so many others had tonight.

"Tommy has known me basically forever," Mason explained.

"I'm kind of like a father figure to him is what he really

means," laughed Tommy. "Mason's trying not to age me in front of a pretty girl, but I would do anything for this boy," he said, kissing Mason on the forehead and ruffling his hair.

I laughed in delight at their banter.

"Let's go inside, my dear," Tommy told me, offering his arm.

I looked at Mason, and he shrugged his shoulders playfully. I grabbed Tommy's arm and we walked inside.

I couldn't help but gape around in amazement. Tommy's house was a museum. There was a little bit of every decade, and every country, sprinkled around the house. One room we passed through appeared to be dedicated wholly to the British monarchy, complete with what looked like an authentic royal crown displayed in a spotless glass case. As we went deeper into the house, I began to hear music playing and a large crowd chattering.

"It must be a real burden to hang out with these two," Tommy said jokingly as we walked into the main room and the girls began to scream with delight at the sight of Mason and Beckham.

"It really is a chore, but someone has to do it," I answered, inwardly swooning when Mason looked back at me and gave me a wink.

The award show festivities had been tame compared to the celebrations taking place right now. There was a huge dance floor in the main room, and couples were going at it in various stages all over. I blushed and looked away quickly when I saw a couple that looked like they could have been actually having sex at that moment a few feet away from where we had walked in. Tommy caught where I was looking and laughed uproariously, slinging his arm around me and leading me to the bar.

"Let's get you a drink my blushing beauty," Tommy garbled, still sounding charming despite his intoxicated state.

"I have just the drink for you to try," he cried. "Alfonso! Make this siren a red-faced virgin."

I gulped somewhat nervously as Alfonso (the bartender), handed me a shot glass with something that was neon green... and smoking. I had brought the shot glass to my lips, prepared to dare a drink, when a hand swooped in and grabbed it from me.

"Hey!" I cried out to the mystery thief. The shot glass was replaced by soft lips. I immediately relaxed into the kiss, Mason's scent and taste washing over me.

A throat cleared near us, and I pulled away reluctantly from Mason. I was really starting to like this whole kissing thing. I turned to look at who had interrupted us, and blushed profusely when I saw that it was Beckham, Vanessa again attached to his arm. Tommy was looking between the four of us, a small grin on his face as if he knew a joke that none of us were a part of. Looking closer at Beckham, there was tension lines around his mouth, as if something was upsetting him. Mason didn't seem to notice.

"Tommy, what the fuck where you trying to give to my girl?" he asked, the shot glass filled with the still smoking liquid gripped in his hand, somehow surviving our kiss.

Beckham grabbed the shot out of Mason's hand and tipped it back quickly, wiping his mouth elegantly with his sleeve. Mason grinned at Beckham, still apparently not noticing the tightness that was all over Beckham's body. He ordered me a drink, this time a glass of champagne, something that I felt much better about drinking. I leaned against Mason as he chatted with Beckham and Tommy, swaying slightly to the music and watching the riotous crowd.

Mason must have noticed my slight dancing because he stopped talking to Beckham and Tommy, and looked down at me.

"Will you dance with me?" he asked in his usual heart stopping manner. I nodded, momentarily caught off guard by his sexiness. Mason kissed the top of my head and strode off towards the dance floor, pulling me behind him. Beckham was following us, Vanessa grasping tightly to his arm. Mason stood behind me and began to move, his body weaving seductively behind me. He was a master at seduction. A brush there, a touch here, all of it served to spin my body to record heights. I could feel the hard length of his arousal behind me. I pushed my body back against it, causing him to curse under his breath. I laughed, looking up at him with delight. I faced forward again... and froze. Beckham was staring at me intensely, Vanessa rubbing up against him almost ferociously. The music seemed to slow, I could sense movement all around me, but in that moment it was just Beckham and I.

We were in a glistening golden room, hundreds of chandeliers and sparkling lights shining down on us. Beckham was glowing, the golden light reflecting off of his hair, making him look more handsome than ever. I was the envy of every girl in the room. He was spinning me around the room as other partygoers danced around me. I was wearing a red, tightly fitted dress that swished around my feet as I moved. Beckham leaned in close to me.

"I've never seen anything so lovely in my entire life," he whispered, so lovingly that I wanted to cry with happiness.

He pulled me into the length of his hard body, a feeling of comfort and rightness welling up inside of me. There would never be anyone else for me.

"Eva," Mason's voice called. I realized I was just standing there on the dance floor staring at Beckham like a creeper. I laughed in a high fake voice. "I think I'm still feeling a little flushed from before the show. Can we go get some water?" I asked Mason, who was looking at me concerned again. I didn't look back at Beckham as we walked off the floor and back towards the bar, but I could feel his gaze follow me off the dance floor. Whatever was going on, I needed to get ahold of myself. Hallucinating about strangers? What was wrong with me?

Four

I made small talk with Mason and some other guests who had crowded around us, as I tried to calm my quaking heart. My hands were shaking just a bit as I clutched my water. I saw Vanessa and Beckham again out of the corner of my eye. She was gesturing to him furiously, her face illustrating her displeasure with whatever he had done. He looked like he felt slightly guilty, but he didn't seem to be saying anything back to her. Tommy appeared out of nowhere on my other side.

"Seems you have your hands quite full, my beauty," he whispered with a wink.

I decided to play dumb even though I could feel my face flushing with embarrassment.

"What are you talking about Tommy?" I tried to joke. He looked at me intently and it felt like he could see right through me in that moment.

"Have you met Damon yet?" he asked randomly.

I frowned, not knowing exactly where he was going with this. "I have..." I responded. "I met him at school."

"Hmmm...and how do you feel about him?" Tommy asked. "It's obvious how you feel about Beckham and Mason."

If I thought I was red before, I now must resemble a cherry. "I...like Damon," I said hesitantly. Tommy smirked at me.

"Is "like" the word you would really use to describe it?" he asked.

I felt a little overwhelmed in the moment. If it was obvious to Tommy that I was crushing on all three of them, then I'm sure that Mason, Damon, and Beckham were all going to catch on to my feelings as well. For someone who had barely been kissed, this situation was quickly spiraling out of my control. I needed air. Now was a good time to go feel the ocean for the first time.

The sounds of the party followed me as I walked outside, desperate for some air and a chance to have a little bit of peace from the people clamoring for attention...and Tommy's questions. Mason was held up with some record executives who wanted to talk about the tour and when the next album was going to come out so he said sent me ahead, telling me he would join me in a few minutes.

Tommy's mansion was literally right on the ocean. It was a full moon tonight, or at least close to it, and the light reflected off the water, lighting my path to the shore. I had left my shoes on the porch and I found myself getting close enough to the water that I could feel the waves rolling over my feet. Since I hadn't experienced the ocean before, I basked in the saltwater smell and the spray hitting my face.

I was much more comfortable away from the prying eyes and the curious questions that everyone had for me about my role in Mason's life. A voice shocked me out of my reverie.

"What are you doing all alone out here?" Beckham's voice floated from behind me.

I stayed gazing at the waves and didn't turn to look at him.

"That was a little bit overwhelming for me," I answered softly. "I'm not used to crowds."

"You would think I would be used to it by now," he replied, almost absentmindedly. "But I still get nervous when I know I'm going to be around a lot of people like tonight."

I looked back at him but he was peering out over the water, seemingly lost in thought. We stood there in silence for a moment.

"You're standing in a fairy ring," he remarked quietly.

I looked up at him confused. He gestured to the sand at my feet. To my surprise there was an almost perfect circle of shells around me. "Oh my! That is so strange. What did you call it? A fairy ring?"

"Yes," he answered. "Fairy rings are said to be good luck and bless the beings who step in them."

I smiled at him and rolled my eyes.

"You don't believe in legends?" he asked, amused.

"I don't believe in fairy tales," I corrected him. Beckham made a noise in the back of his throat in disagreement. He took a step closer to me and placed a hand on my waist. I could feel the heat from his body enveloping me.

I was standing in mother's rose garden, reaching out to pick one of her famous hybrid ones, when I felt someone approach me from behind. I relaxed when the smell of pine and fresh musk enveloped me.

"Hello my love," Beckham said softly, brushing his lips against my neck.

I smiled and turned around, wrapping my arms around his neck and pulling him close. "You came," I exhaled. He kissed me like he hadn't seen me in years. His tongue sliding into my mouth, licking and tasting me like I was his favorite treat. I pressed against his lips, devouring his lips in return. He was my favorite flavor and every kiss was better than the last. He pulled back from me, his gorgeous grin darkening briefly.

"Father kept me longer at my studies," he answered apologetically. *"He had some sort of meeting with your father in the king's private chambers this morning, and was late to my lessons. I thought about you all day though."*

I sighed at his sweet words.

"Do you know what they were meeting about? Father would not say," he asked.

I frowned with a little bit of frustration.

"Mother says we have an important guest arriving soon," I answered, shrugging. *"She won't tell me who though. I'm sure it's just another emissary from one of the kingdoms, nothing to be bothered about,"* I smiled reassuringly.

"I won't stop being bothered by it until you are my wife, my love. I fear your father is going to marry you off one day to one of these ambassadors you worry so little about," he teased, tapping me on the nose.

"It will never happen," I responded fervently. *"We're not only a love match, but we have been fated by the Gods. Not even my father can argue with that. We just need to wait a bit longer, my birthday will be here soon."*

Beckham looked down at me intently, seeming to be memorizing my promise.

"Forgive me for worrying my angel. Shall we go for the walk I promised you?" Beckham asked sweetly.

I gave him a peck on the lips and took his hand. As we began to walk I looked behind me, feeling like I had forgotten something. When I looked back, I noticed that a small portion of the roses just past where I had been standing seemed to have withered, something I had never seen in our land. I made a note to tell mother about it.

I jerked forward, stepping away from Beckham's touch, blindsided by the image I had just seen. Now was not the time for me to be daydreaming, although it had seemed more than that. Like what I had experienced before the show when I had fainted, and what I had just experienced while I had been on the dance floor with Mason and Beckham, the images I had just seen seemed more like a memory than anything else. I was confident though that I had never been to wherever I was in my dream, and I certainly had never met Beckham before today. Curious.

"Everything all right, Eva?" asked Beckham, sounding concerned at the abrupt way I had pulled away from him.

"Yes, sorry, I thought I felt something on my leg," I said lamely.

I still did not want to look at him. I felt overwhelmed at what I had just seen, and the feelings it had brought to the surface. In whatever I had been seeing, Beckham had been mine, as familiar to me as one could ever be. I touched my lips, almost surprised that they weren't swollen from the kiss he had given me. My cheeks flushed involuntarily.

"Eva," Beckham said softly, stepping beside me so that he was in my line of sight. "Why do I feel like I have known you my whole existence? Tell me you feel this...this whatever it is between us. I feel like you've returned to me, although I don't know where you went. I..."

Whatever he had been about to say was stopped by a voice calling out my name. Mason was walking towards us from the mansion, strands of his long hair whipping in the breeze, his shirt sticking to his chest, outlining his perfect pecs and six pack. He had taken off his suit. I knew that he hated being dressed up, he had complained enough in the limo about the "monkey suit" he was wearing. He was looking delicious in a fitted white v-neck tee and black jeans.

I looked back at Beckham, so beautiful in his own right. More silver than gold under the light of the moon, he was still wearing the slim fitted grey suit he had worn to the show. Both would inspire any woman to immediate devotion. My heart fluttered in my chest. I really was falling for both of them. And then there was Damon...

"You two okay?" Mason asked, looking between Beckham and myself. "Vanessa is looking for you Beck, she seems in a mood so I would approach cautiously," he joked.

Beckham gave a small grin.

"Yes, I should be getting back to the party. You are going to stay at my place tonight right? I know you don't want to drive all the way back to your place tonight since it's already so late."

"I had rented a hotel room right near the show, but I guess I wasn't thinking about how far away the after-parties would be," Mason answered sheepishly. "I guess it makes sense to go to your place."

"Good," answered Beckham, pleased. "Let's leave soon, these people are exhausting," he said, walking backwards back towards the party, looking somewhat longingly at me before turning away.

Mason was quiet, staring out at the black waves, deep in thought.

"Beckham's been one of my best friends since almost before I can remember existing," he said quietly, still not looking at me. "I would give him almost anything. But if he wants you, I'm not going down without a fight."

He finally turned to look at me, a question in his eyes. I didn't say anything. Instead I took his hand and kissed it softly, laying his palm against my cheek and savoring its warmth. Mason dropped the subject and pulled me into his arms. We stood there quietly for several minutes, both staring out into the water, each lost in our thoughts.

Five
Beckham

My stomach was in knots. More of the strange images featuring Eva had floated through my head throughout the night. I was old enough, had experienced enough, not to believe in coincidences anymore. I knew these images meant something, that they possibly could be real memories, I just didn't know when they were coming from. Unlike Mason and Damon, I didn't know what I was, only that I seemed to be immortal since I had been hanging out with them for a few hundred years now. The only power I had seemed to exhibit was one of persuasion. It differed from person to person, but for the most part I could convince anyone to do anything I wanted. It even worked on Mason and Damon, although I had made a vow to never use it on them after they had been furious at me after I made them pretend to be chickens once in front of some beautiful nymphs.

I tried to search my memory for any point in time that seemed to be missing, but there didn't seem to be any gaping moments absent that I could find. I knew I could never voluntarily forget someone like Eva so there had to be something more at play. She already felt indispensable to me, like she was a part of my body that I could not live without. I sighed as I walked up the back deck stairs, up to the party. My head ached...and so did my heart. Of course Mason and I would fall in love for the first time in our existence, and it would be with the same woman. We usually didn't even have the same tastes in women. I had never contemplated this being an actual problem. I felt guilty. I already knew that Eva would be worth throwing away eons of friendship to have her, but I hoped that wouldn't be the price.

Vanessa was waiting for me by the back entrance into the party.

"Where were you?" she asked. "I've been looking for you everywhere."

I sighed and pulled a hand through my hair. "Just taking a breather from the party," I answered with what I hoped looked like a nonchalant shrug. "You know how I am about these things."

She nodded. She did know. I had been taking her to these events off and on for at least three years, and she knew I never enjoyed myself. Vanessa looked past me, out to the water. I knew she would see Mason and Eva still out there. She frowned when she did.

"Beckham...you had said you wanted to have a talk with me tonight about us," she said slowly.

I let out a sigh. I had wanted to avoid this conversation. I'm just glad we hadn't had the original talk I had planned at the beginning of the night, before I had met Eva, because then this would have been even worse. "Vanessa...I care about you..." I began.

"Stop, Beckham," she said softly, tears gathering in her eyes. "You were actually going to give us a chance weren't you? But then you met her."

I didn't know what to say, and my silence must have said

enough. She put a hand on my face, seeming to be memorizing it. "Vanessa, I still value our friendship immensely. I don't want to lose that." I said meaningfully.

"Beckham. I can't be friends with you anymore, at least not for a long time. It hurts too much. I've been living for the moments I've been able to see you for the last three years. I haven't dated. I haven't even been able to look at another man. Please just do this for me. If you can't love me, please just leave me alone. But I should warn you...a girl like Eva is going to break your heart."

I stared down at her and finally pulled her into a hug, brushing her forehead with my lips. Vanessa had been there for me for all the craziness of my career and had been a good friend. But Eva...I knew with my whole heart that she would eventually become my everything. I would lose everything at the chance to be with her if I had to.

Vanessa stood on her tippy-toes and kissed me on the side of the mouth before turning to leave. Knowing what I needed to do, I pulled Vanessa to me so that she was facing me, and looked in her eyes.

"Vanessa. You are no longer going to have romantic feelings for me, and from this moment on I will not even be a thought to you. You will forget that we were ever friends. You will return to your home and feel at peace."

I didn't want to add the part about forgetting we were ever friends, but I felt that it was safer than running the risk she would continue to want to hang out with me and would fall back in love with me. I watched as Vanessa's pupils dilated.

She looked confused for a moment before shaking her head and looking up at me with confusion.

"Sorry, I must be a little bit drunker than I thought. Hope I didn't bump into you too hard," she said.

"No problem, it's a crowded room in here."

She looked at me for another moment before smiling and

saying "Bye!" in a friendly voice. I watched her walk away, a little bit of sadness welling up inside of me at losing such a good friend.

Mason and Eva had just walked up the stairs after Vanessa left. "Ready to go?" I asked them. Mason looked a little upset and Eva looked pensive.

"Let's go," answered Mason gruffly.

We went to find Tommy to say goodbye. He whispered something in Eva's ear that made her blush before Mason pulled her away from him, giving Tommy a clap on the back before walking away. I saluted Tommy and turned to walk away as well.

"Beckham," said Tommy, calling after me.

I turned to look at him in question.

"She's not a girl you let slip away," he said.

For someone who seemed drunk ninety-nine percent of the time, I couldn't deny that he knew what he was talking about. I nodded my head and headed out after Mason and Eva to where the limo waited for us.

Six
Eva

Beckham's house was exactly what I would have picked for myself...you know, if I had millions of dollars at my disposal. His home looked like it belonged more in the Hamptons than Malibu. Beckham called it a "beach cottage" but it was almost 7,000 square feet. It was made out of white stone and dark brown wood beams, and it had a huge lap pool with an accompanying pool house. It took up a few acres of the beach, giving Beckham the privacy he wanted when he wasn't on location. Everything was white inside with light grey ash wood floors.

I stared around in amazement. Every place I went to in my strange new world was better than the one before. There was a moment of awkwardness when Beckham asked where I was sleeping. Mason looked at me with hopeful eyes, but I just couldn't stay the night with him, especially in Beckham's home. My skin felt electrified from the continual touching both had done all throughout the night. I had gone from unwanted touches from Mr. Anderson that disgusted me, to having three men that lit my soul on fire touch me constantly.

I felt overwhelmed after the visions that I kept seeing, or

whatever they were, and needed some time alone to go over everything. Mason looked disappointed but gave me a sweet kiss before letting Beckham show me to a guest bedroom.

The bedroom that Beckham brought me to looked like something out of every girl's fantasy. There was a giant gold mirrored headboard on a king size bed, covered by a lacey white duvet cover.

"This doesn't look like a man's room," I laughed as Beckham showed me around.

He flushed.

"My designer made a few bedrooms that would appeal to a more feminine taste," he explained.

There was a giant window seat with a fluffy white cushion and gold pillows that looked out towards the ocean. There were black and white cursive quotes in gold and black frames all around the room. My favorite one was a quote from Helen Keller that read "Life is a daring adventure or nothing at all." The room was utter perfection.

He showed me an ensuite bathroom with a large separate tub and another fancy shower that had so many knobs, I wouldn't know what to do with it. I oohed and ahhed at everything he showed me until we were done with the tour, and Beckham was hovering by the door.

"Thank you for letting us stay here," I said awkwardly. "Your home is perfect in every way."

Beckham glowed, as if I had given him a huge compliment.

"Can I get a good night hug?" he asked charmingly. His hair was ruffled, and his eyes looked tired, but he still looked so, so sexy. I stepped into his embrace, basking in his scent of pine and musk, a scent that seemed so familiar to me like everything else about Beckham. I felt him kiss the top of my head and take a deep breath, as if he was absorbing my scent as well. I pulled away, afraid that I would have another one of those strange visions, and smiled at him. He stared at me for a second before slipping out the entryway and shutting the heavy wooden door behind him. I took a deep breath, and let out a sigh. Having the attention of these men was so overwhelming.

Beckham had a drawer that was filled with various products that fit the potential needs of any woman. I examined the various bottles and tins looking for anything that seemed familiar. After washing my makeup off with some face soap I had found, I changed into the pair of boxers and an oversized shirt Mason had lent me to sleep in. I crawled into the large bed and sighed. It was the most amazing bed I had ever encountered. My dorm bed was obviously a huge step up from the army cot the Andersons had me sleeping on for years, but this bed was the most comfortable thing I had ever experienced. Feeling like I was sleeping on a cloud, combined with the excitement of the day and night, I drifted off to sleep almost immediately. As soon as I closed my eyes I dreamed.

I was over the moon after my afternoon with Beckham. He was the sweetest, most wonderful man in the whole world, and I couldn't wait to start my life with him. I ran into the Queen's suite where a servant had said my mother was, so I could tell her all about it. I felt the change in the air as soon as I stepped through the entryway.

The mood was somber, and everyone was uncharacteristically whispering. One thing about my mother was that she exuded vitality. She was the life of every party, every room, every conversation. People loved my mother, Queen Eibhleann, and for good reason. She was beautiful, with golden hair and porcelain skin. She had the same amethyst colored eyes as the queens in our line always did. Everyone said that I looked just like her, but I didn't think so. To me, mother was the loveliest, most perfect being that ever existed, and I was so glad that we lived forever so that I would never lose her. I walked back to my parent's chambers, wondering why everyone was acting so strange.

My mother's chambers were all white with accents of lavender and gold that closely resembled her features. My mother was laying in my parent's enormous bed, her hand strewn across her eyes, a wet silk cloth across her forehead.

"Mother?" I asked inquiringly before crawling into the bed to lay close to her.

My parents had waited a few thousand years to have me as my mother had struggled to conceive as all our people had as of late. We had always had a close bond, and she never let me forget that I had been a priceless gift from the Gods. She moved her head to look at me, her beautiful eyes looking tired and dull.

"Hello my love," she said.

"Are you all right? It isn't like you to be in bed so early in the afternoon," I asked.

"I've been feeling weak the past few weeks. It's nothing to worry about. I'm sure I will feel better with a little rest. There has been much to deal with in the kingdom as of late," she told me.

"Can I help with anything?" I asked.

Mother was very firm that I be brought into the kingdom's affairs slowly. Her mother had passed away suddenly and mother always talked about how she would never forget how stressful and terrible it was to have so much responsibility and power at such a young age. Although I had heard whispers from others in the court about the power I was already displaying, one that rivaled my mother's already, she had allowed my progression as a ruler to evolve naturally. I was tutored and listened in on certain meetings, but I was still allowed a lot more freedom than father felt I should have. But he never won any conversations about me. The power in the land was with the queen, and no queen had ever been as powerful as my mother.

"No my sweet," she replied. "I will let you know if the time

comes when I need you to take on more responsibility. Now enough about that, I can tell you have been with Beckham because you are absolutely radiant. Tell me all about it."

Mother loved hearing about Beckham and I since she wasn't living her own love story. Mother and father had not been a fated match, and though they seemed to get along well, I could always feel an air of unhappiness around her when when her marriage was brought up. My father, King Gealtaire, had been the son of a regent in the summer realm, one of the powerful provinces to the east. When my grandmother passed so suddenly, the kingdom had been in an upheaval as my mother was still so young. Mother's advisors had begged her to agree to marry someone who would strengthen her reign. Mother had agreed for the sake of the kingdom. Father was older than her, and provided an air of stability to her image. Although she seemed to have made the best of their union as she and my father had managed to be married peacefully for thousands of years, I wondered if she ever regretted it. I couldn't imagine not being with Beckham. I shook my head at my thoughts and eagerly went into the events of the afternoon, pushing the worry aside for now. We lived forever. That wasn't going to change now. Everything would be fine.

I awoke the next morning still wrapped in the sensation of the love that I had felt radiating from the beautiful woman in my dream. I laid in bed for awhile, staring out the window at the waves crashing against the shore, going over all of the dreams I had been having lately, and the...visions. Vision seemed to be the only word that could describe what I had seen yesterday around Beckham.

I was fast coming to the conclusion that I would have to stop ignoring all of the strange things about myself, and what I had been seeing since I met Damon, Mason, and Beckham. Growing up, I had always wanted to just be... normal. Even if it meant ignoring what was right in front of my face, whether it was my freak healing abilities, my ability to master almost any new skill, the intense feelings (whether it was hate, lust, or love) that I engendered in everyone. I always told myself everything would be alright if only I didn't think about it. But I couldn't ignore it any longer that something was wrong with me.

I was an aberration, a freak. I wondered if no one knew where I came from because I had been some sort of science experiment gone wrong or something.

I laid there for a few minutes, trying to find peace in the sound of the ocean and the seagulls floating in through the window I had left open the night before. I eventually decided it was rude to laze the morning away feeling sorry for myself when I was a guest, and that I needed to get up. I also had the desperate urge to be around Beckham and Mason. They helped fill the empty hole inside of me that seemed to be growing wider the more revelations I discovered about myself. I wanted to bask in Beckham's smile and melt into Mason's kiss. Although let's be honest, I wouldn't mind kissing Beckham either. And then there was Damon as well...

I made my way into the bathroom and finally figured out the shower after a few minutes of fiddling around with the knobs. When I came back out into the bedroom wrapped in the fluffiest, softest towel I had ever felt, there was a gorgeous crimson sundress laid out on the bed in my size along with matching sandals. While I wondered at how Beckham had known my size, I wasn't going to argue with such a gorgeous gift. I blushed thinking about Beckham being in my bedroom while I was in the shower naked.

I slipped into the dress, and ran a comb that I had found in Beckham's magic toiletry drawer down my hair. I opened the door and started walking down the long hallway to where I thought I remembered the kitchen being. I still couldn't get over the size of all the places I had been lately. Between

Damon's penthouse, the hotel suite in L.A., Tommy's mansion, and now Beckham's "cottage," I felt like I had experienced the lap of luxury.

As I got nearer to the kitchen, I heard deep voices discussing something back and forth. It sounded like Mason and Beckham. I stopped near the entrance to the kitchen when I heard my name.

"Have you been able to tell what she is?" Beckham asked. "Is she a succubus, or perhaps some kind of vampire? She certainly has the sex appeal of both species," he continued.

"She's definitely not either," Mason replied. "If she was a succubus she would have a similar energy pattern as I do, and I haven't seen any sign of vampiric traits."

Mason hesitated for a moment.

"Honestly Beck, her energy pattern is similar to yours, just on a much higher frequency. She might be whatever you are."

Beckham huffed.

"Well that's helpful since we know so much about where I came from," he muttered.

"She doesn't seem to know what she is," said Mason. "How is it possible that she could have lived her whole life not knowing that she's more than human?" he asked. "And if she really doesn't know, it would mean that she really is just 18," he said with a little wonder in his voice.

Beckham interjected.

"Didn't you tell me she was just about to turn 18? Did you miss her birthday? You know that 18 is usually the birthday..."

I stopped listening at this point, my mind churning over the information they had divulged. I could care less about my birthday as I had never had anyone celebrate it with me before. The only reason it was a little important this year was because it meant legally the Andersons would have no right to me.

What was actually important at this moment is that

Mason and Beckham had basically said they were creatures I had only read about in fairy tales, and that I probably was one too. I wanted to believe they were crazy with talks of succubi, vampires, and the like, but it honestly sounded more palatable to me that there was a supernatural reason for my abilities than that I was a crazy science experiment that was grown in a test tube like I had been thinking earlier. My heart sped up and my hands got clammy. I should just go in there and confront them about what I had heard, but I was too nervous.

I decided to creep back to my room when I noticed the voices had stopped. I felt a whoosh of air in front of me and all of a sudden Mason was staring back at me suspiciously.

"How long have you been standing here Eva?" he asked, not bothering to make an excuse for the fact that he had basically just appeared in front of me. "You should have just come into the kitchen. Breakfast is ready."

"I just got here," I answered brightly, both of us knowing that I was lying.

Luckily Mason didn't press me on the issue, instead, he pulled me in for a kiss that left me aching.

"I missed you last night," he whispered in my ear.

I melted into his embrace. Supernatural or not, this man had been nothing but amazing to me. I couldn't find it in me to be afraid of him, or Beckham for that matter. I suddenly thought of the extraordinary skills that Damon had shown. Obviously he was more than he seemed as well. I felt overwhelmed. I just escaped an attic for goodness sakes and the first men I meet aren't even human. Figures.

SEVEN

I walked into Beckham's gorgeous farmhouse style kitchen that had stainless steel appliances that looked like they belonged on a spaceship, Mason following behind me. I stopped abruptly however when I saw Beckham standing shirtless, in a low hanging pair of navy sweatpants, flipping pancakes over the stove. Looking at him now it was obvious he had to be supernatural. I had never seen anything so delicious in my life. Well I guess since the last time I looked at Mason or Damon I laughed to myself. Beckham was an in between of Mason and Damon, all golden skin stretched taut over perfect muscles, and I swear he had an eight pack (even though I had read that wasn't possible in one of Mrs. Anderson's Cosmopolitans I had stolen). Mason came up behind me and wiped at my mouth.

"Just wiping away the drool," he teased me.

I blushed, but didn't deny I had been checking out Beckham. Who wouldn't when faced with a body like that. He literally looked like he had been carved by the gods. How could I ever have thought for a moment the two of them were just normal men?

Beckham's gold hair was tousled perfectly like he had just rolled out of bed. He still looked sleepy, and my mind began to wonder if that was what he looked like when he first woke up... Mason cleared his throat, still staring at me amused. I blushed even more if that was possible, then attempted to nonchalantly walk past Mason to pour myself a glass of orange juice from a pitcher that was sitting out on the counter. I tried to slip past Beckham, but he spun around and caged me in. I stared nervously at Mason, wondering what he thought of the situation. Mason was eyeing Beckham and I closely, but seemed to be waiting to see what Beckham was going to do.

"Sleep well angel?" he asked me, pressing his hips slightly into me.

His touch, combined with his hard length, felt like it was drugging me, but I stirred to attention from his use of the endearment "angel." Hadn't that been what he called me in my dream? I lost my train of thought again when he leaned his face in close to mine, our lips almost touching.

"Are you still asleep?" he asked smiling.

I wanted so badly to lean in the inch remaining and brush his lips with mine, but I stopped myself.

I became very aware that Mason was still watching us. I could feel his heightened energy even standing a few feet away from him. It was hard to tell however if he was upset or not. I stepped to the side, dragging my body away from Beckham. It literally felt like torture. That connection that I had felt from the second I had laid eyes on him seemed to be growing stronger every minute. I smiled at him, feeling bad that me pulling away from him had caused his face to fall.

"I must still be asleep," I said apologetically. "Are you really making pancakes though or is this a dream? Because feel free to wake me up like this anytime you want." I said, clumsily trying to flirt.

Beckham's face fell back into its easy going grin.

"Is this how I get your attention? Just make some pancakes without a shirt?" he laughed.

Mason spoke up from the other side of me, surprising me since I hadn't even noticed that he had moved.

"If that's the case, I'm cooking breakfast," he said, making me giggle and gasp in a weird way. The weird sounds I was making escalated when he too whipped off the v-neck he had been wearing. He then cuddled up to my side, his naked chest pressed against me. I could feel the heat creeping up my neck. I was sandwiched between two of the hottest guys in existence.

Mason was covered in tattoos. His chest didn't have a single blank space. It was hard to tell what was what since everything overlapped. I did recognize an angel wing tattoo going up the top part of his chest, and the phrase "lust over love" written in cursive over his heart. That was an odd phrase to choose to have on your body forever. I would have to convince him to let me take a closer look at all of his tattoos. I idly wondered if he had tattoos on other parts of his body and if I would ever get the chance to see those... Mason coughed and I saw that Beckham was openly laughing at how flustered I obviously was. Mason backed away and went to the stove, taking over pancake duty just like he had threatened. I didn't think my ovaries were going to survive this trip.

I quickly moved away to the large island and pulled out a chair, slowly sipping the juice that Beckham slid over to me, trying to calm down. I admired the muscles in Mason's back as he fiddled with the stove. I could feel Beckham's amused eyes still on me.

"Are we leaving soon?" I asked Mason, trying to think of something to say, feeling awkward from overhearing their conversation and being surrounded by all of their sexiness.

"Do you have practice this afternoon?" he asked.

"We have off until tomorrow since today is the last day before classes," I replied.

"You should stay for a few hours then," said Beckham eagerly. "We could drive up the coast," he added.

"Could we spend some time on the beach?" I asked timidly. "Last night was my first time being on the beach."

Beckham and Mason exchanged glances.

"Of course," Mason answered me.

Excited for the beach plans, I went back to ogling Beckham and Mason while they finished making breakfast. Soon Beckham handed me a plate loaded with eggs and pancakes. I eagerly dug in. I had been too nervous to eat very much so far this weekend. Mason poured me a cup of coffee. I took a sip and grimaced. Mason laughed at me.

"I guess I got used to a certain kind of coffee I always get in the city," I replied, groaning inside at the fact that once again I was covering up my connection with Damon.

"Have you tried this place called Leslie's?" asked Mason.

I froze, not knowing what to say.

"Yes," I said slowly. "That's actually one of my favorite places," I said.

Mason stared at me with a searching look but didn't say anything more much to my relief. A cell phone on the kitchen counter started ringing, interrupting the moment. Mason picked it up and glanced at it, looking perturbed.

"Yes?" he answered, sounding impatient. "I have plans today," he spoke to the mystery caller. "Why does it have to be done today?...Fine, I'll be there in twenty," he finished, cutting off the speaker without saying goodbye. "Fuck," he swore, tossing his phone on the counter.

He looked at me forlornly.

"I've got to run to a meeting with the record executives at the label before we leave this afternoon. Beckham will have to keep you occupied."

I looked at Beckham. He was wearing a huge grin on his face like he had just found out he had won the lottery. I felt nervous all of a sudden. I was sure that Beckham's presence was the catalyst for all of the strange visions and dreams I had been having on this trip. I wasn't sure that I wanted to have more this afternoon. Beckham's face dropped when he saw the unease on my face.

"We can go wait at the recording studio for Mason to get out of his meeting if you want," he said with a sad look.

"No, I'm excited for our plans," I announced, trying to ease his mind.

Mason looked between the two of us, and then shook his head before walking over to me and kissing me soundly on the lips.

"I'll see you in a few hours," he said. "Don't have too much fun without me."

I smiled and hugged him for a moment, feeling his smooth skin against mine, before allowing him to pull away from me to leave. I watched him walk out of the room before turning towards Beckham who had been watching the two of us avidly.

"Where to first?" I asked with a grin.

Eight

The rest of the morning was magical. After we put the dishes from breakfast in the sink, Beckham led me down another long hallway to a garage that had a multitude of shiny cars, trucks, motorcycles, and the like. It resembled the garage under Damon's penthouse, except I knew that all of these vehicles had to belong to Beckham. Although, come to think of it, Damon probably owned most of the vehicles in that garage as well since he hadn't let Shelton answer my question about the cars the other night.

I was cut off from my distracted musings when Beckham clicked a key, and the most gorgeous white convertible beeped from nearby and started automatically. I decided right then and there that it was my dream car.

Beckham laughed at me when I involuntarily squealed with delight, and did a little jump. He opened the door and waited for me to get in before walking around to the driver's side. One of the garage doors opened, and he sped out, making me look frantically for the seat belt before I flew out of the car.

It was a gorgeous day. I was convinced that the sky was just more blue in California. There was a light breeze in the air that pulled at Beckham's hair as we drove, making it dance. He looked more like a golden prince than ever before with the strands glistening in the sunlight. That same bittersweet sense of familiarity rushed over me and I had to look away before I involuntarily started to tear up for no explainable reason.

I watched fascinated as we drove down a highway that ran parallel to the ocean. I was in awe of it all. The smell of the sea in the breeze, the squawking of the seagulls as they dipped and dived over us, the sound of the waves crashing against the surf, it was so different than New York City, but no less magical to me. I looked over at Beckham who for some reason looked extremely masculine in that moment casually steering with one hand. He had put on a pair of aviators like the male models I had seen in magazines, except he looked a million times sexier than any of them had looked.

I sighed and he glanced over at me, an amused look on his face.

"Enjoying yourself angel?" he asked. Why did that endearment sound so familiar as well? It was making me feel like I was going crazy, this sense of deja-vu when I knew I had never met him before. I must have been showing my frustration on my face because he casually grabbed my hand and started rubbing his thumb over my skin in a soothing manner, not seeming to care that I hadn't answered his question. I laid my head back against my seat and stared back out at the ocean, trying to ignore the ever present tingles flowing up my body from where we touched, the same feeling I always got when I was near any of the guys.

We drove for at least an hour, chatting back and forth about nothing in particular, when he pulled off to the side of the highway that opened up into a scenic lookout.

"We're here!" said Beckham excitedly as he popped the trunk and hopped out of the car.

He grabbed a basket and a blanket that I hadn't seen him

put in the car, and then came around to my side and held out his hand for me to grab.

Beckham led me down a set of steep stairs that I hadn't noticed descending from a break in the guardrail. I gripped the railing and Beckham's hand tightly, and picked my way down the metal stairs, not looking up at the views until we had reached the bottom. When I did look, I gasped in amazement. We were standing in a gorgeous, little beach that was completely deserted. It was like Beckham had transported us to a private paradise where we were the only two people who existed.

The water was a perfect deep blue with waves that crested softly against the gilded sand. There were white shells scattered along the shore with the occasional strands of seaweed. Beckham had set down the basket and blanket and was now watching me keenly, with that same amused smile he always seemed to be wearing.

I couldn't help but give him a sudden, huge hug in delight. Of course a hug wasn't enough for him, he immediately used the close proximity to scoop me up in his arms and start to run towards the waves.

"Beckham, no!" I screeched, alarmed at the fact that I was pretty sure he was about to dump me in the water.

He was sweeter than I had given him credit for though. When we got to the water's edge he put me down, sliding me down his body slowly as he did so, staring into my eyes. His gaze was so intense, so filled with unspoken words, that I couldn't even be distracted by the touch of the icy water against my toes.

"Angel," he whispered, reaching up to brush a strand of my hair from off my face.

"Beckham, stop!" I squealed with laughter as he continued to chase me through the trees. He kept up his pursuit, letting me stay far enough in front for it to still be fun. I burst through a

break in the trees suddenly and found myself at the edge of the lake. I stopped before I hit the water and admired the view in front of me while I waited for Beckham to catch up. It was a gorgeous day, the sky a glistening blue that reminded me of Beckham's eyes. There was a breeze floating off the lake, carrying with it the scent of fresh honeysuckles from across the way.

All of a sudden hands grabbed me, and I yelped in surprise. It was Beckham of course, and I sighed with delight when he scooped me up in his arms and twirled me around before setting me down. As he slowly slid me to the ground, our eyes met. The years of sly flirting, and stolen touches seemed to bubble up between us in that moment. He stared at my lips, momentarily entranced by them.

Would this be the moment, the moment that carried us beyond the best friends we had been for years? The moment that fulfilled the fate's promise that we were a soul match... Beckham slowly leaned towards me, his supple lips softly caressing mine. That seemed to be enough to spark a fire in him however, as he suddenly crashed his lips into mine with a fervor I hadn't seen from him before. I melted into the kiss, feverishly tasting him back. His hands softly caressed me, holding my head in place as he kissed me deeply. This was surely love...

"Eva," Beckham said sharply, slightly shaking me at the same time.

I just stared at him, my mind whirling over what I had just seen. What was happening to me?

"Eva are you all right? You've been out of it for a full minute!" he said.

At least I hadn't fainted this time as we appeared to be in the same position we were in a moment before.

"Yes, yes. I'm fine," I assured him. "I don't know where my head's been at lately," I lamented.

He looked at me suspiciously.

"Are you sure you're alright?" he asked.

I suddenly wondered if he had seen the same thing as me.

"Have you noticed anything strange since we met?" I asked him cautiously.

"You mean besides the fact that you seem to have trouble not fainting around me?" he asked, finally relaxing and letting out a laugh. His laugh was belied by a nervous twitch at the corner of his eye. I frowned, frustrated at all the mysteries in my life at the moment, and the fact that neither he nor Mason seemed to want to volunteer what they knew. Although I couldn't really talk since I hadn't mentioned Damon to either of them...

Beckham turned and began leading me towards where he had dropped the picnic basket and the blanket, his arm draped around my waist. He pulled his arm back to spread out the blanket and I immediately felt the loss of it. I sat down and pulled my knees up to my chest, going over what I had seen.

Was I dreaming about another life? Was this one of those things I had read about where people were reincarnated or something and I was seeing one of my former lives? It was either something like that or I was going crazy because the feeling that I had known Beckham for perhaps forever was growing stronger.

I idly watched Beckham begin to pull out strawberries, fancy looking cheese, and some cut up French bread, wondering when he had time to put such a nice basket together. We picked at the food in silence, not necessarily an uncomfortable one, just a distracted one. I played with the sand next to the blanket, going over everything I had seen in the last few days. First things first though...I needed to ask Beckham about the conversation I had heard this morning between him and Mason. But how did you go about asking about vampires and succubi... with a straight face?

"I heard you this morning," I blurted out.

Beckham's eyes bugged out, and he choked on the strawberry he had just put in his mouth.

"What exactly did you hear?" he asked, seeming to be trying to choose his words carefully.

"This sounds crazy coming out of my mouth...but I heard you talking about how I wasn't exactly human...and that you weren't either."

Beckham stared at me for a moment.

"You're taking this awfully calm considering most people would think you were in the presence of a lunatic after hearing something like that," he finally answered in a measured tone, the slight shake in his hands the only way to tell he was caught off guard by my statement.

"There's always been something off about me," I said reluctantly.

I really didn't want to get in to what had happened to me at the Anderson's, but I at least had to explain some of it for him to understand what I meant.

"Where I lived before," I began. "They weren't exactly kind to me. The woman, Mrs. Anderson, she actually seemed to hate me. She learned early on in my stay there that I seemed to recover very quickly, actually much more quickly than anyone else I have heard of."

Beckham's face had turned a pale ashy color and he looked sick at what I was telling him. I hurried on before I lost my courage.

"It started small, with just basic bruises disappearing quickly after she gripped me too tightly. Then I think she started to experiment. In the end she liked to burn me more than other things."

He opened his mouth, but I continued on, wanting to finally get it all out.

"It wasn't just healing though. It was things like my hair too. She hated it for some reason and one of my first nights there she hacked at it, practically tearing it off rather than cutting it."

I stared off into the water now, remembering the feeling of dread I had looking in the bathroom mirror after she had cut all of my hair off.

"I remember running my hands through my hair. It was cut so short that I just knew it would take years to grow back. I went to bed that night distraught, but when I awoke in the morning, it was all back."

I took a deep breath.

"Strange things like that have happened throughout my life. I suppose it's a relief to have something to attribute it to, rather than just thinking I am some kind of freak."

I finally glanced away from the water and dared to look at Beckham. His face was one of rapt attention.

"You said that she...that she burned you. I assume then that she also made you bleed?" he said inquiringly.

I wondered why he would ask that specific question, but answered anyway.

"Well actually, no. I have a condition. I think its fairly mild, but it must have scared them enough the first time they cut me that they were careful to never make me bleed again."

"A condition? What kind of condition?" Beckham asked me quickly.

"My file says that it's some kind of hemophilia. But I apparently eventually stop bleeding since I'm still here," I answered, laughing a bit self deprecatingly.

"You don't have hemophilia, Eva," he stated emphatically.

"What do you mean?" I asked.

"For a supernatural, our blood holds a great deal of power. Did you see anything strange when they cut you? Can you not think of any other time when you have bled?"

I wracked my brain and realized I really couldn't think of

any other time where I had bled. I couldn't even think of a time when I had fallen and scraped my knee.

"I passed out when they cut me after the blood started falling," I said slowly. "And no, I can't remember ever bleeding before. That can't be normal," I said, starting to feel a bit hysterical.

Beckham pushed the food aside and moved closer to me, stroking my arm reassuringly.

"Everything is okay, Eva," he said sweetly. "Supernaturals are not exactly known for being clumsy, so it would make sense that you couldn't remember having any sort of accident that would make you bleed. If that woman..." he paused, seeming to need to get ahold of his emotions for a moment. "If that woman cutting you was truly the first time that you had been cut, then the rush of power released from your blood could very easily have caused you to faint. I'm sure it scared those monsters to death."

He paused, seemed to be lost in thought.

"I do wonder why your file would have said you had hemophilia though."

He shook his head and tipped up my chin so that I was looking at him.

"I know this is a lot to take in, but I will try to answer whatever you want to know," he told me, seeming so earnest that I felt like I could trust him with anything in that moment.

"So obviously you and Mason are also...supernatural," I said, the word supernatural feeling awkward in my mouth.

"Yes, we both are," he answered, looking concerned that I was going to bolt at this.

"But you don't know exactly what you are?" I asked hesitantly.

"You were listening to quite a bit this morning weren't you, angel?" Beckham said with a smirk.

I blushed and looked down, a little bit ashamed for having eavesdropped so much.

"But yes, my background is a little bit of a mystery. I seem to remember back for at least a thousand or so years it seems, but I have no idea where I came from, or what I am."

"And Mason thinks that we could be the same?" I asked hesitantly.

"Yes. Mason has the ability to read energies to a certain extent. Every living thing emits some kind of energy, but those of supernatural origin emit energy on a different frequency. Mason can tell the difference between all of us."

"What is Mason?" I asked. "Does he know?"

At my question Beckham tensed up a bit.

"That's not really my story to tell," he said, looking decidedly uncomfortable.

I wondered what Mason could be that would be a big enough deal that Beckham didn't feel comfortable telling me himself. I decided to let the matter drop since I had about a million other awkward questions I wanted to ask.

"Do you have any special skills?" I asked, wondering if I had something similar since I could be the same thing as him. Beckham again looked uncomfortable.

"My gift seems to be that I can be...persuasive," he answered, looking away from my gaze.

"Persuasive. What exactly do you mean by that?" I asked uncertainly.

"I mean that I haven't met a single person...or supernatural, who doesn't do exactly what I tell them," he answered, with a very serious face.

I thought about what that meant for a moment. I couldn't imagine that kind of power. If I had something like that I could have avoided so much of what had happened in my life. I pulled my knees up closer to me and wrapped my arms around them. So far it seemed the only "superpower" I had was the ability to heal from extreme abuse. A rush of jealousy flooded me.

"I don't have anything like that," I said, a little bit of pain leaking through my voice. Beckham again stroked my face and leaned in close.

"You haven't turned 18 yet have you?" he asked.

"No," I said, confused at the question. "I turn 18 in three weeks."

"For most supernaturals, their powers don't truly come in until they turn 18," he explained.

Immediately a rush of hope flowed through me. Not that I had ever dreamed of having superpowers or anything like that, but the idea that I could have something to make me not so vulnerable and weak was infinitely appealing to me after everything that had happened in my life.

Beckham's phone went off suddenly, causing me to jump a little bit. He picked it up and read whatever text had come in.

"I'm sorry to end this conversation, but Mason is back at the house waiting for us. Your flight is going to leave soon."

I looked around at the beautiful place Beckham had brought us to and felt a rush of sadness at the thought of leaving it...and Beckham.

Beckham helped me stand up, and we picked up the food and blanket and started to walk towards the stairs that led up to the car.

"We need to actually go swimming next time," he said, grasping my hand as he led me up the stairs.

"Next time?" I asked.

I couldn't help but feel a little hope at his words. Beckham didn't say anything until we finished climbing the stairs. He turned to me.

"Eva, I feel like you are everything I've ever been looking for in my life and didn't know that I needed. It wouldn't be possible for me to let you go."

I felt tears glistening in my eyes at his statement. I felt the same way. That he was somehow my "home." My thoughts turned to Mason and Damon. Although my feelings for Beckham felt more familiar for some reason, what I felt for them was just as strong. Beckham must have read the indecision in my face.

"I'm not asking you to make a choice now, I'm just telling you that if there's a race for your heart, I'm all in and I'll never not be all in."

He took one last step towards me, and softly grazed my lips with his. It didn't feel like a first kiss I realized. It felt like he had been doing that for all my life. Beckham's phone went off again with a text from Mason asking if we were on our way yet. Beckham finally led me to the car. We were both silent on the way back to his house.

Nine
Mason

I watched Eva's face as we walked onto the plane to head back to New York. We were on my smaller jet this time as a few members of the crew had needed to leave for New York this morning to start getting ready for the next concert. Her eyes lit up with the same awe and delight as they had with the larger one. I loved seeing her reaction to everything I introduced her to. Thankfully, we had a different flight attendant working this jet, and not Eliza again. I needed to remember to move Eliza to somewhere else so I could avoid more awkward run-ins with her. I had never minded having my former fuck buddies around, but now that Eva was in my life, I wanted to avoid that as much as possible. She had definitely suspected something had gone on with Eliza, but had been sweet enough not to give me a hard time about it on the way to California yesterday.

Beckham had pulled me aside when she was grabbing things from the room she stayed in, to tell me that she knew what we were. I had known that she had heard us this morning, and the fact that she hadn't run screaming from the house had made me confident enough to be more open with some of my abilities in front of her. It was still a relief however that Beckham was the one who had the conversation with her. Beckham had a way of making everything seem better and nicer than it actually was. I would have fucked it all up. I was also grateful that he hadn't told her what I was. I felt like once she knew, she would want nothing to do with me.

It didn't inspire much confidence in my ability to be a stellar boyfriend when a girl found out that I was an incubus. It was partly why I had never been able to be a totally faithful boyfriend in the past, not that I had ever tried to be one. I hadn't found a female supe that I could tolerate for more than a one-night stand, and a human girl couldn't have survived how much energy I needed if she was with me all the time. It was one of the reasons why Courtney had been perfect. I could get what I needed while on the road, and could see her just enough to be able to feed on her without hurting her.

Eva was different though. I had told Beckham that her energy level was similar to his, just on a higher frequency, but I hadn't told him just how high her energy level actually was. I hadn't encountered anyone with the kind of energy levels she was giving off. I could actually feed off her energy quite easily just being around her, I didn't even have to touch her. I hadn't come across someone with that kind of energy before. Those kind of energy levels seemed to suggest that she was going to be very powerful when she came into more of her powers.

I wanted her to be able to trust me while I played the Europe leg of my tour. One of the reasons that I always chose to be a musician in whatever era I was living in, was that I could feed on the crowd with the emotions that my music stirred in them. It would be a little rough not also getting energy from sexual sources, but it was possible. I would just be weakened. Eva would be worth it though. And hopefully I wouldn't have to go the whole tour without seeing her.

There wouldn't be time for me to come back in between

shows, but I didn't know if I could make it three months without seeing her. Not because I needed to feed, but because my soul felt like it had withered just being without her this afternoon. Ugh, I sounded like a fucking sap... Maybe I could surprise her and fly her to my Paris show, and she could stay for a few days. I knew Rothmore had some kind of fall break, I would have to find out from Damon what it was.

I groaned inwardly. Maybe I wouldn't find out from Damon. I knew there was something going on between him and Eva even though she had tried not to mention it. I had known it as soon as she mentioned that Leslie's was her favorite place to have coffee. You didn't find a place like that in New York by accident. It had to have been Damon who introduced it to her, and Damon had never brought a girl there before. It was bad enough that Beckham seemed to be ready to marry her, but it made my stomach sick to think about Damon and I falling in love with the same girl. I had called him my brother for what seemed like a millennium and I never would have dreamed that anything could get between us, let alone a girl. I thought about how lost Damon had been when I had met him. He had never been truly happy since I met him, always pining away for the paradise that he had lost. Of the three of us, Damon was the one who needed Eva the most. But with the way I felt about her...I just couldn't bring myself to let her go.

I looked over at Eva. She had been quiet since her afternoon with Beckham. She was staring out the window as we took off, seemingly lost in thought. I decided I needed to talk to her about the tour and see where she stood with things. She had been kissing me back, but she hadn't instigated anything, and I knew I was competing against Beckham now and probably Damon as well. I just hoped she would let me have a chance to win her heart. I took a deep breath.

"Eva, we need to talk about my tour."

She looked up at me alarmed.

"Okay, what do you want to talk about?" she asked hesitantly.

"I have the European leg of the tour still to go. I'll be gone for at least three months," I said nervously.

Eva's face had gone blank.

"So we probably won't see each other again you mean," she said stiffly. "I didn't expect for you to even talk to me past the after-party the other night. I understand how it is."

"Wow...no, shit...that's not what I meant," I said, stunned at how little she seemed to care. "I want to talk to you as much as you will let me. I would bring you with me if I didn't know how much starting school meant to you," I said meaningfully.

Eva's eyes had filled with tears, and her face had softened.

"Oh," she said. "I didn't expect that."

"Eva, I'm crazy about you. Surely you had some clue of that? You've turned my whole life around," I told her.

She shuddered a little bit and I stood up and scooped her up in my arms, walking us over to one of the many couches situated on the plane. I sat down and she cuddled against me. I smoothed her hair back, she still hadn't said anything about how she felt.

"Do you like me at all, love?" I asked, immediately feeling stupid for sounding so insecure and vulnerable.

She looked up at me. "I like you a lot...I just have no experience with this sort of thing," she said hesitantly. "But I need to tell you something," she continued.

I tensed up, expecting the worst.

"I am starting to have feelings for Beckham as well...and Damon," she said, looking ashamed.

I hated the words as soon as they came out of her mouth. I wanted her to love just me, but I couldn't say that to her.

"I just want a chance to win your heart, Eva," I said softly. "The feelings I'm starting to have for you are once in a lifetime, give up everything you have, do anything you want me to do kind of feelings. I'm in this to win it."

She sat up and looked into my eyes. I held my breath, waiting anxiously for what she was going to say or do. She held my eyes as she leaned in, pressing her lips softly against mine. I took that as a good sign and immediately strengthened the kiss, wrapping my arms around her and pulling her tight against me. I licked at her lips until she opened her mouth so that I could taste her. I groaned. She tasted so sweet.

Eva tentatively brushed her hands through my hair, pulling it out of the bun I had thrown it up in. My hands slid down her sides, careful to stay in safe places. I didn't want to scare her even though I wanted her so bad it was hard to think.

I lost track of time as I kissed her. I savored each brush of her lips against mine, knowing I would have to survive without it for what would feel like an eternity. Finally, she pulled away, smiling shyly at me. I leaned in for one more kiss.

"Are you hungry?" I asked her, realizing it had been hours since she had probably eaten anything.

"Yes I am," she said, looking surprised at the thought.

I laughed at her look, and then pressed an intercom next to the couch to ask for an attendant to bring us dinner. Within minutes, one of the staff came in with two trays. Eva politely thanked the man as he set down the trays. He blushed profusely, and almost dropped everything.

"It's not a problem, miss," he said with a slight stutter.

He hurried away after seeing the warning look on my face. I sighed.

"I don't think I'm ever going to get used to everyone's reaction to you," I said exasperatedly. "I try to take it as a compliment rather than being jealous, but fuck...you are too pretty for your own good."

She blushed charmingly in the way she always did when someone complimented her.

"I don't know why they look at me," she said.

I stared at her stunned.

"You're kidding right? You must know how gorgeous you are. I've never seen someone like you."

She was quiet for a moment.

"I've always known that there was something about me that caught people's eye, I'm not completely oblivious," she said. "But its never been a good thing. The people that I was with before this...they told me that the devil was inside of me. That I was responsible for all of the bad things that men...and sometimes women...wanted to do to me. I haven't ever been able to think good things about myself."

A rush of hate so great that I could have choked on it flowed through me. It had been obvious to me since I met her that she had a past. The more I found out, the more I wanted to rip apart everyone who had ever hurt her. Eva should have been worshipped her entire life, and instead she had obviously been abused and mistreated in the worst kind of way.

I tipped her chin up so that she would look at me.

"You are a gift Eva. The whole world should be grateful to receive even a glimpse of you, and should be bowing at your feet. I feel like I have been blessed a million times over to have even gotten to spot you in the crowd at the concert. Even if I had never seen you again, it would have remained the most significant moment of my life up to that point."

I kissed her again softly and tasted the tears that were now streaming down her face. She didn't say anything in response to my statement, instead picking up her fork and beginning to pick at her food. After eating, she curled up next to me, and we watched a movie that I had put on one of the screens. I soaked in the moment, wishing it would last forever.

Ten
Damon

A cold fury had spread throughout my body. I had turned on the tv to watch the Grammy's, knowing that Mason was performing. Funny enough, all anyone could talk about was the mysterious, gorgeous blonde on Mason's arm that was not Courtney Rayne, his girlfriend.

Something inside me had known at that moment that it was Eva, but I hadn't wanted to believe fate could be so cruel. I sat on the edge of the couch, drink in hand, and waited for them to show his date on the screen. I didn't have to wait long. There she was. Looking so fucking stunning in a black dress that I couldn't breathe. He had his arm around her, leaning into her ear, and making her laugh. I didn't know how this was possible. Mason had been in town for two days, and Eva had just spent the night with me.

How was it possible for her to be close enough for him to take her to the fucking Grammy's as his date? Suddenly, I remembered her stilted words the night before. How she had mentioned a kiss. Mason had kissed Eva. It felt hard to breathe, the room was stifling and seemed to be spinning. Mason had been my fucking brother for centuries upon centuries. I had thought I would give him anything, that I would do anything for him. But obviously I had a limit. She was mine. I wasn't going to share her. He could have anything else, but this was the only thing in my life I actually wanted. She was my redemption.

My hands were shaking. I walked swiftly to the bar area, grabbing whatever was out, and pouring myself a large glass. Mason was about to perform. I watched in horror as he kissed her summarily on the lips before getting up to go backstage, like he had been fucking doing it his entire life. Like she had always been his. I threw my glass at the tv at that moment, shattering the screen. I overturned the coffee table next, desperate to get out the rage that was all-encompassing. I felt betrayed. I knew I hadn't even kissed Eva yet, but I thought she knew we were heading towards something. And then she picked Mason? Was this my punishment for the shit that Selena had pulled? It wasn't going to happen. Eva was mine. Mason could go to hell.

Eleven
Mason

I was already feeling anxious after dropping off Eva at her dorm room. I had wanted to walk her in, but she didn't want me to get mobbed by the coeds that were out celebrating their last night of freedom before classes started. I had kissed her until she started laughing and pulled away. Watching her walk away felt like a piece of my body was leaving with her. Her blonde hair reflected the light coming from the campus lights, making the gold in it flash brightly. And her ass as it swayed as she walked...she was perfect. I didn't know how I was going to make it through the rest of the tour. I usually lived for touring, but now it was the last thing I wanted to do. I looked out the window moodily as the city passed by silently.

The car pulled up in front of my building. I slipped out without waiting for the driver to open the door and hustled inside, pulling my hat down low. It wasn't uncommon for photographers to camp outside of our building trying to get a picture of Damon or I, and I didn't feel like dealing with them tonight. Luckily I didn't see anyone, and I was able to get through the lobby to our private elevator without any issues. I wiped a hand down my face. Fuck, I was exhausted. I hadn't slept at all the night before since I was so wired from the show and being around Eva. Sleeping down the hall from her when I could have had her in my arms had been pure torture. And now I wouldn't know what that felt like for months. Hopefully, I would just have to get to the Paris show I recited to myself, trying to ease my anxiety.

The elevator smoothly slid to a stop and opened to the penthouse. I walked in, eager to get to my bed, but stopped suddenly. The penthouse was destroyed. Our beautiful tv was laying in pieces on the ground in the living room, with a huge hole in the wall behind it. Glass was everywhere, and the sofa had been overturned. What the hell had happened?

I entered further into the room warily, listening for an intruder. All I could hear was the clinking of ice cubes on the outdoor balcony however. Fucking Damon. I bet this had a little something to do with seeing Eva on the TV with me at the show last night. He had told me he was going to watch. Of course at that point I didn't realize that anyone other than Courtney was going to be on my arm, and Damon was more apt to feel sorry for me about that situation than anything else.

I took a deep breath and cracked my neck, prepared for the shit show that was about to begin. I wondered if maybe I could just sneak back out and camp out on Lane's couch…

"Welcome home…," came a sarcastic voice from outside.

I walked out to where I could see Damon leaning over the balcony, several bottles from our liquor stash scattered on the ground around him.

"Have fun in California?" he continued, in the same annoyingly crass tone.

"As a matter of fact I did," I answered. "The best time actually."

He snorted but said nothing in return.

"Look, Damon…let's talk this over. I didn't know that you

even knew her until I had already started falling for her," I said, deciding just to get this over with.

Damon said nothing. He turned back towards the skyline, staring intensely out, as if the city could provide answers to the situation.

"I haven't been truly happy in so long that I've begun to think that happiness was actually a myth that I had imagined. They ruin you, you know. That's the worst part about falling is that you once tasted paradise. And because you tasted paradise, it's impossible to be able to settle for anything else because you know what you are missing out on. But when I'm with her...that feeling that I've had for thousands of years, that feeling that I'm immeasurably lost, that I'm doomed...it disappears. I feel...complete. I didn't think that was possible for me."

He was silent for a moment as I absorbed his words. I didn't know what to say. I felt as intensely about Eva as Damon did, just in a different way. I had never held the same emptiness as he did, but I felt like Eva had been specially made for me. Besides how lovely she was inside and out, I didn't have to actively feed around her. I could just be normal, just a guy in love that didn't have to think about where my next fuck was going to come from, and if I would go too far and hurt whoever I fed from. It was a freeing feeling.

Damon might have thought that Eva was his redemption... but she was my redemption as well. As much as Damon and Beckham were the only people I had ever met that I considered family, I knew that Eva was on her way to becoming immeasurably more important to me.

"You know it ultimately isn't up to us," I said finally.

Damon glanced over to me.

"Eva gets to pick. She told me..." I took a breath, not wanting to admit it out loud. "She told me that she was falling for all of us."

"What do you mean all of us?" Damon asked, puzzled.

"She and Beckham connected on the trip," I admitted glumly. "Beckham is head over heels for her already as well. I saw him looking at the script of "Lucky Break," that movie that's being shot in New York that he had told us he wasn't going to take. Looks like he's going to take it now after all because of her."

"What the ever loving fuck," exclaimed Damon. "It's literally been two days."

He turned on me.

"Did you use your sex power on her?" he asked in an accusing tone.

I looked at him incredulously.

"You're shitting me right? I wouldn't do that to her."

Damon groaned.

"I know. It's just painful to know that I made less of an impression on her in a few weeks than you and Beckham did in less than 48 hours."

"I don't think it's like that," I said slowly. "As much as I don't want to admit it, I think it's eating her up inside that she cares about Beckham and I at all since she feels so strongly about you. But Damon, I told her I'm all in. I'm going to fight for her no matter what you say or how you feel."

Damon had turned his back on me again.

"Fair enough," he said. "But this isn't something I'm going to lose."

His giant charcoal wings flew out suddenly, tearing his shirt, and almost smacking me in the face. He was about to leap off the balcony when I decided to drop the even bigger news that had come out of the weekend.

"Eva knows what we are."

I watched amused as he tripped a little from shock. He looked at me angrily.

"Great job idiot. Is she terrified now and wants nothing to do with us?"

"She actually handled it really well," I answered. "She doesn't know what we are though. Beckham was kind enough to leave that part out."

He grinned all of a sudden, looking much more positive than he had looked before.

"I can't wait until she finds out you're an incubus," he said, practically giddy.

He leapt off the balcony without another word. I watched him with a sick feeling in my stomach as he sailed off into the night.

Twelve
Eva

It was everything that I could do to hide what I was feeling from Mason by the end of the trip. I kept my back stiff and my walk steady as I got out of the car and walked back to my dorm. I could feel Mason's eyes on me, and the last thing I wanted was for him to follow me in because he thought something was wrong with me. He had been so wonderful to me, but somewhere between the airport and arriving at my dorm room, everything that had happened in the past forty-eight hours had finally sunk in. And it had been more than my poor mind could take.

I had gone from never interacting with anyone and spending my time locked in an attic for four years, to being around thousands of people. My skin was crawling, and not in the tingling way that it did whenever one of the guys touched me. My heart was racing, and I was having trouble breathing. Once I got inside the main door and out of Mason's view, I practically ran to my dorm room, throwing the door closed behind me and collapsing in a heap on my floor, trying to stave off the panic attack that was bearing down on me.

While the crowds and contact had been overwhelming in

themselves, finding out that I wasn't human, and that the men I was falling for weren't human, had tipped me over the edge. I had consciously avoided talking about that issue with Mason. I had thought that I was handling it alright after my conversation with Beckham. He had been so patient with all of my questions, but the more I thought about it, the more fractured I could feel my mind become.

I had always known there were monsters in the world, the Andersons and many others in the foster system had taught me that, but finding out that I was most likely an actual monster was overwhelming. I counted out my breaths, focusing on breathing in and breathing out slowly even though my body was trying its best to hyperventilate. Tears slid down my face. I was being stupid. Hadn't I loved snuggling with Mason? Hadn't I felt safe wrapped in Beckham's arms on the beach? Why was this just hitting me now? I needed to pull myself together. Classes started the next day, and I was not going to show up to class having a fit, or worse yet, miss my classes all together because I was freaking out.

I laid on the floor for who knows how long before I decided to try crawling towards my bed, my limbs shaking, and my breathing still coming out in gasps. I tried to pull myself up to my bed, but I was breathing so fast at this point that I couldn't pull myself all the way up. I felt a sudden rush of air behind me and then strong, familiar arms lifted me onto my bed. Damon was here.

"Please don't touch me," I called out, sobbing.

"What's wrong? What can I do?" he asked, panic threaded through his voice.

I didn't answer him. I just shook my head. I was now hiccupping from how hard I was crying and my body had started shaking as well.

Damon had immediately let go of me when I asked him to, but the shaking must have been too much for him to watch without trying to do something. He carefully laid down next to me, folding me into his arms. I had thought that I didn't want to be touched, but his familiar warmth had the immediate effect of grounding me and stopping my shaking.

His hand slid through my hair softly, and he began to talk in a gentle tone about random things. I couldn't concentrate on his actual words, but the smooth cadence of his voice calmed me. His voice sank into me, relaxing my body, and soon I found myself falling into a deep, dreamless sleep.

I woke up the next morning, the mellow light of dawn streaming in from my window. Damon's arm was wrapped around my waist, his face nestled in my neck. I turned as slowly as I could so I could look at him. He looked so calm asleep. Damon was normally so intense, always moving and full of energy. I hadn't gotten to see him asleep the night I had been at his place, so I felt like I was getting a rare treat.

"I can feel you staring at me," he said all of a sudden with an amused voice.

I blushed, even though he hadn't opened his eyes yet, and flopped on my back.

"Hey, come back. I was snuggling," he said, in an adorable voice, finally opening his eyes and looking at me.

I got lost in the emeralds of his eyes for a moment, getting reacquainted with their beauty. It seemed like I hadn't seen him in forever. A rush of regret flowed through me at the way I had left him the other night. Even with that, he had been so sweet last night, gifting me with sleep that I for sure wouldn't have gotten if he hadn't been around. Except...how had he gotten in my room?

"So, I think you are the sweetest boy ever for taking care of me last night...I'll just preface my question with that first," I said hesitantly. "But how exactly did you get in my room?"

"I heard that you and Beckham had a conversation about the three of us on your trip this weekend?" he asked.

"Yes," I answered hesitantly.

"And he didn't mention what exactly I am?" he asked.

"No," I answered, suddenly nervous.

"It might be easier for me to show you," he said. "First, promise you aren't going to run from the room screaming though."

Well now I was very nervous. What if he was some kind of shifter like in werewolf books, and I had a gigantic wolf sitting in my dorm room? I backed up slowly towards the wall and pulled the covers up to my neck.

"I'm ready," I announced.

Damon laughed at me uneasily. He slowly stood up and faced me, situating himself in the center of the room. Suddenly there was a loud crack, like Damon's bones had all broken into pieces. Two enormous, charcoal colored wings burst from behind him. They extended to each side of my dorm room, taking up every inch my room had to offer.

I couldn't help but gasp. Damon was some kind of angel I was guessing? Majestic didn't do a good enough job of describing how striking and impressive his wings were.

He looked at me shyly.

"Well," he said tensely. "Do you think I'm hideous?"

I pulled down the covers and crawled off the bed, walking towards him. I reached out a hand to stroke one of his feathers before pulling my hand back abruptly.

"Am I allowed to touch them?" I asked.

He looked surprised, and then hopeful.

"Yes of course!" he said quickly, taking a step closer to me to allow me better access.

I brushed my hand against the edge of one of his wings. Up close I could see that there was actually silver threaded throughout the charcoal feathers. They were breathtaking.

Damon shivered as I continued to stroke him.

"Am I hurting you?" I asked.

"No, baby. Let's just say that my wings... are very sensitive," he said with a sly smile.

I blushed, immediately knowing what he meant...But I didn't stop stroking his wing. I was fascinated by it. It made Damon look that much more masculine, like he was a god that had come out of the pages of a mythology book about the creation of the world. Suddenly I wanted him to know how "un-scary" I found him. I wanted him to know just how much I appreciated all he had done for me since we had met, how sweet he had been.

I took a step closer, moving slowly so that Damon could see what I intended to do. He held his breath and watched me, his tongue peeking out and slightly moistening his lush lips as he waited with anticipation to see what I was going to do.

I moved my hands away from his wings and touched his chest. I realized that he hadn't had a shirt on at all since he had come to visit me last night, and I greedily took an opportunity to admire his sculpted chest and abs, running my hands all over them. I looked back up at him and stood on my tippy toes, delicately brushing my lips against his. He took a deep breath in and then pulled back suddenly.

"Are you just kissing me because Mason or Beckham aren't here right now?" he asked, vulnerability leaking out of his words.

"I'm kissing you because I'm falling for you, and I'm so appreciative you are in my life," I answered meaningfully, holding his gaze in the hope that he could see how earnest I was being.

Damon studied my face for a moment.

"I'll take whatever you are willing to give me," he muttered before sweeping me into his arms and kissing me so passionately that I lost my breath.

"I want you to know every part of me," he said after

pulling back from the kiss. "I'm going to prove to you that I can be everything you need."

I opened my mouth to object. It wasn't that Damon was lacking, it was that all three of them held a different part of me. One couldn't replace the other. He didn't let me respond however.

"It's your first day of college," he said excitedly. "I know you probably have a million questions for me, but I'm going to go get us coffee from Leslie's while you get ready, and then I'm walking you to class. We can talk about everything else when it isn't your first day of school."

He kissed me again hurriedly, and then left the room, actually using the door this time before I could even get a word out. I touched my lips, now swollen from his attention, and idly wondered if he realized he didn't have a shirt on. There were bound to be heart attacks around campus and the city when people saw. I laughed to myself, feeling so much better than the night before, and excitedly started getting ready for my first day of college.

Thirteen

Damon was back within thirty minutes, fully dressed in a navy v-neck and ripped jeans, carrying two steaming cups of Leslie's coffee. I was already ready, just finishing brushing my hair out when he knocked on the door. I had chosen denim shorts and a red off the shoulder blouse for my first day. I hoped that it wasn't too casual. I knew that most of the students here were very wealthy, and I could imagine them all in sweater vests or something equally stuffy.

Damon placed the coffees on my desk and walked over to me, reaching out to touch my cheek gently.

"You are so beautiful," he breathed out before kissing me briefly. "Can I just tell you that I'm really glad we are at the kissing stage now," he said with a laugh. "I have been wanting to kiss you since the moment I saw you."

I blushed.

"I'm glad too," I answered affectionately.

He handed me my cup of coffee and looked around my room.

"Are you ready for class? What do you have first?" he asked.

With my free hand, I picked up my backpack that I had put my supplies in the week before, after finalizing my class schedule.

"I have three classes today," I answered. "First up is Art History at 9:00am, then Intro to Psychology at 10:45am, and then I have Statistics at 2:00pm."

"Perfect, we can have lunch together after your 10:45 class," Damon said. "I mean, if you want to have lunch," he said hurriedly, after I raised my eyebrows at him.

I laughed at him affectionately.

"Of course I do," I answered. "What classes do you have?"

"Well, I have Art History at 9:00am, and then Advertising and Promotion at 10:45am," he answered. "So I guess I will get to experience your first college class with you this morning," he said with a wink.

I let out a breath I didn't realize I had been holding. I had actually been really nervous about starting classes, but with Damon at my side I had nothing to fear. Damon grabbed my bag from out of my hand, and slung it over his back. I laughed at the picture of my masculine Damon carrying a pink backpack on his shoulder. He winked at me again, and I melted a little. He grabbed my hand and we walked out of my room and the dorm together.

It was a gorgeous day, the leaves around campus were starting to change, and there were bursts of crimson, burnt orange, and gold everywhere you looked. Students were everywhere, hurrying to and fro, yelling out greetings to one another after a summer apart. I soaked it all in, acknowledging that a few months ago I couldn't have even dreamed that I would have this opportunity. Having this chance meant so much more to me than going to the Grammy's or mingling with stars.

As usual, people were staring at us as we walked along, but I attributed it more to Damon's presence than my own. Damon had put on a pair of Ray Bans, and despite the pink backpack on his shoulder, managed to look the epitome of cool. I sighed inwardly at the fact that his lips had kissed me earlier.

As we walked I had a thought.

"Isn't it a little unfair that you play football?" I asked. "I mean you can fly...I'm sure there's some inhuman strength and speed mixed up in there as well."

He laughed, looking chagrined.

"So this is embarrassing...but there's actually a pill that Mason and I discovered that has a dampening affect on supernaturals. I take it before games so that I'm playing more on a human level," he explained. "Thousands of years would be pretty boring if we couldn't interact with humans at all, and I've always been obsessed with sports or things related to sports."

I shook my head in understanding, musing on what he had just said. Thousands of years caught my attention more than anything else. It was one thing for them to casually mention how old they were, but it was quite another to actually imagine it.

Suddenly I heard a squeal, and I was knocked to the side as a body collided with mine. It was Lexi, looking her usual beautiful, boisterous self in a pair of artfully torn jeans and a black tanktop.

"Eva, babe, you look gorgeous," she exclaimed.

As usual she didn't wait for me to respond, hurrying along.

"Wasn't this weekend amaaaazing?" she said. "I can't believe we are already starting classes! What class do you have first?"

Damon was staring at Lexi in shock, I think more amazed

at how many words Lexi had managed to get out in so short a time than anything else. I told Lexi my schedule and she squealed again.

"I have statistics too!" she said excitedly. "We can walk to practice together afterwards!"

My heart leapt a little at finding out I had another friend in a class. This day was going to be even better than I had imagined. Suddenly a group of girls passed by, one of them yelling "slut" at Lexi and I. I looked around shocked, and saw that it was Selena and her group. Lexi recovered quickly, flipping them off and telling them to "fuck themselves." The girls hurried off, looking appalled at Lexi's behavior. Damon chuckled beside me.

"I like her," he told me.

I grinned.

"Me too," I answered.

Lexi hurried off in another direction after a few more minutes of walking with Damon and I, pushing it to make it to her class on time. We walked up the concrete stairs into an imposing red brick building named "Abravanel Hall." I squeezed Damon's hand harder as we walked into a large lecture room where at least a hundred students were milling around, chattering with one another. The room went silent as people began to notice us. I saw Eric to my left. He had been sitting with a bunch of what looked like football players, but he had stood up upon seeing me.

"Eva," he called out, gesturing me over, and looking relieved to see me. I didn't really want to sit next to him, but I still felt like I owed him since he had been the first friend I had made here. Damon sighed as I led him over to the group, but didn't say anything. I realized we were still holding hands when I saw Eric staring, but wisely Eric chose not to say anything. Eric reached out to give me a hug, ignoring the little growl that Damon gave under his breath.

"I tried to get ahold of you a million times this weekend," Eric said. "I wanted to apologize about last week."

I took my backpack from Damon and began to rifle through it, trying to stall for time. I wasn't sure how to explain where I had been this weekend. Luckily for me the professor, a thin, distinguished looking man with the most amazing mustache I had ever seen, walked into the room.

"Everyone get seated please," he announced as he began to pull books out of a leather briefcase he had laid on the front desk.

I gave a small sigh of relief, and Damon let go of my hand, giving it a final squeeze before he settled himself into the seat next to mine.

The hour passed quickly with the professor providing an overview of the class, and a brief explanation of the art periods we would be studying. I stared enthralled at the slides the professor went through, slide after slide of stunning artwork, each with a much deeper meaning than I would have guessed at first glance. With the exception of the professor staring a little too hard at me while calling roll, it was the perfect start to my college experience. I was so caught up with everything that we were going over that I lost track of time and was surprised when the professor announced class was over.

I looked over at Damon. He had been doodling throughout class. I supposed if you were an ancient being, studying art that you had probably seen in its original time period just didn't compare. Still, I was grateful that he was in the class with me, and that I would be able to pick his brain about pieces that he had seen in real life. I got up and began to start gathering my things. I felt a soft touch on my elbow. Before I even looked up I knew it was Eric.

"Do you want to go to lunch with me next?" he asked me, giving me a pleading look.

"She actually has class after this," said Damon stepping

around me, and taking my elbow from Eric to start leading me out of the room.

"She *actually* can speak for herself Damon," Eric snapped at him.

The rest of the football players were watching the scene with trepidation. I was sure that they didn't make it a habit of starting problems with Damon. Damon stopped walking towards the door and turned. He glowered at Eric, holding eye contact with him until Eric finally looked away. Damon then took my hand again, and we proceeded to walk out. I looked back. Eric was staring at Damon with so much hate that it put a shiver down my back. He would need to be dealt with soon. At the very least his attitude towards Damon needed to stop if we were going to stay friends.

The rest of my first day of classes passed uneventfully. I liked my second class just as much as my first. I was interested in psychology and why people behaved the way they did, and thought the class would be a great introduction to the field. Damon was waiting for me outside of class and again walked hand in hand with me to the lunch hall. I got the usual stares, with the addition of some jealous glares from various girls we passed by, but besides that we were left alone. My third class was my most fun class of the day surprisingly. I had always hated math, but Lexi kept me laughing the whole time and surprisingly seemed to be really good at Statistics, always knowing the answer despite not seeming to be listening at all.

After class, Lexi and I walked to cheerleading practice. I tensed up as we got closer to where the team was gathered. I was sure there was going to be repercussions from Selena for the attention I was getting from Damon and Mason. I was sad that something I had been so excited about had already become something that gave me so much anxiety.

The fallout started as soon as Lexi and I stepped foot on the field. Selena had decided to freeze me out, and had gotten a lot of the team to follow suit. Lexi muttered curses at them every chance she got while I tried to ignore the fact that most of the girls were acting like I didn't exist.

We were practicing a pyramid routine when the next part of Selena's plan went into action. Coach Ryan had put me as the flyer even though it felt like I was too tall for the role based on YouTube videos I had been watching of routines. We had practiced this routine a little bit the week before, and everything had gone off without a hitch. This time however I had butterflies in my stomach as we started.

Selena had a huge grin on her face when she looked over at me, like she knew something that I didn't. It was hard to concentrate as her devious grin reminded me of the one she had flashed me at Damon's the other night when she was butt naked and on her knees. As we approached the part where I was hoisted to the top, I saw her give a nod to someone below me. All of a sudden the hands gripping my ankles let go, and I toppled towards the ground. Right before my face crashed into the ground, what felt like an invisible cushion seemed to appear in front of me, and my descent stalled. After a second I fell again, but this time only from an inch away, so I wasn't injured at all.

I laid there for a second in shock, listening to the girls yelling back and forth. I had no idea how I was going to explain what had just happened to the team. I couldn't even explain it to myself. I should have had a broken leg or worse. I sat up slowly. Lexi had gotten to me first, freaking out hysterically and patting me down.

"Eva, are you okay?" she said, her voice catching with emotion.

"I'm fine," I said reassuringly, pretending to stretch out my arms and legs to check for injuries.

Coach had run over to me, talking quickly into a walkie-talkie in her hand. She stopped suddenly in shock when she saw me moving around.

"Never-mind," she spoke into her handheld. "Eva, how are you feeling?" she asked.

"I'm fine," I said again. "I hit some girls on the way down so it broke up my fall," I told her, trying to think up a plausible excuse for what had just happened.

After seeing that I was okay, Coach seemed to get furious, immediately turning around and yelling at Selena and some other girls for their "carelessness." Selena was looking at me like I was the one who had done something wrong, but her friends around her looked shaken up. Weirdly it didn't appear that anyone had seen me stop right before hitting the ground. Surely they would be saying something about it right?

Lexi grabbed my hand and helped me up, brushing dirt off of me.

"Are you sure you are really okay?" she asked me again searchingly, staring at me as if she could see my secrets.

I smiled in response and gave her a side hug.

"Perfect, it wasn't that far of a fall."

Lexi didn't seem convinced, but luckily let it go. Coach didn't seem to be over what had happened, and called an early end to practice. I strode off the field with Lexi, aware of a dozen girl's eyes on my back as I walked away.

Fourteen
Damon

I waited outside of Eva's dorm room for her to get done with practice. I could tell she wasn't used to having a phone since she seemed to never have it on her. Mason and Beckham had both been texting me throughout the day wanting updates on how Eva was doing since she wasn't answering their texts and calls. I had begrudgingly given them short answers, jealousy rippling through me as I did so. I had decided that I was going to attempt to play nice. Mason's speech and the depth of his feelings had softened me somewhat. Additionally, Eva would definitely be turned off if I let the raging jealous idiot inside of me show, so for now I needed to act relaxed.

Finally, after what seemed like forever, I saw Eva walking with Lexi towards me. I immediately knew something had happened. Lexi looked near tears, and Eva had a very serious look on her face. I jogged to meet them.

"What happened?" I demanded.

"Your ex happened," said Lexi with a glare.

I groaned internally. Selena was going to be one of the biggest mistakes that I had made in my very long life. But looking back, how could I have prepared for someone like Eva? I couldn't have even imagined someone so perfect existing in the world, let alone that she would like me.

I took Eva's hand and pulled her towards me, smoothing the hair back from her face.

"I'm so sorry baby," I said quietly.

"It's not your fault," Eva said fervently. "Some people are just awful and nothing can change that."

Lexi must have decided it was time for her to leave, because she pulled Eva away from me to give her a big hug.

"Call me if you need anything," she demanded, her smile subdued.

Eva squeezed her in return, and Lexi walked away, not before giving me another evil glare of course. Eva started walking into her dorm, waiting by the door for me to catch up.

"Did you remember Mason's concert tonight?" I asked her since she hadn't said anything about it yet.

"Oh no!" she exclaimed.

She began to pat her shorts, looking for her phone in pockets she definitely didn't have in her tiny cheerleading shorts. I got momentarily sidetracked when I noticed how amazing her ass and legs looked in them. She looked up chagrined and started laughing, the stress of her practice seemingly out of her head.

"I forgot my phone today," she said still laughing. "I'm just not used to having one."

I kissed her on the top of her head as she unlocked her room door, and we walked inside. She walked to her phone and started scrolling through the messages that people had left. She blushed as she read through them. I involuntarily rolled my eyes, sure that most of the messages were from Beckham or Mason. I didn't ask about them though, which seemed to me to show pretty great restraint since most guys would freak out about their girlfriend getting texts from other guys. Girlfriend...I mused on the word. Technically I hadn't asked her to be my girlfriend yet, but with the way I felt about her, it didn't seem strong enough of a word.

Eva set her phone down and went to the closet. She started rifling through the clothes that were hung up. I absentmindedly looked around her room, admiring how she had brightened up the place. I had never liked a lot of color in my home but I found myself wanting Eva to do this in my penthouse. Of course that vision also included Eva living at my penthouse with me, something that I was still set on making happen. I heard a door closing, and turned around. Evidently Eva had shut herself in the closet to change. I laughed.

"Everything okay in there?" I asked.

"Just changing," she said in a muffled tone.

"You know I could have just closed my eyes," I snickered.

"Uh huh," she said, like she doubted my eyes would stay closed.

This immediately made me start thinking of her naked... which made my body react accordingly. I don't think I would survive that if or when it happened. She already was perfection with clothes on...

My musings were cut off by her opening the closet door and stepping outside. She looked gorgeous as usual, wearing some kind of off the shoulder white blouse with a jean skirt.

"Ready to go?" I asked, checking my phone and seeing the concert was going to start soon.

"Yes!" she said excitedly.

I took her hand as we stepped outside of her room. I would never take for granted getting to touch her.

Shelton was waiting for us out in front of Eva's dorm. We got in the car and began to drive towards Metlife Stadium. Eva was quiet while we drove, and I could tell that she was thinking deeply about something. I signaled Shelton through the reflection in the rear-view mirror to put in his headphones so Eva and I could have a private conversation.

"Baby, something on your mind?" I asked gently.

She looked over to me and smiled, but it didn't reach her eyes.

"You're being awfully wonderful about the fact that we're going to your friend's concert after I spent the weekend with him," she said quietly, a guilty look on her face. "We didn't talk about it this morning. I'm sure a part of you hates me right now. I don't know how you have even been able to be so sweet to me. I don't deserve it."

I knew I needed to choose my words carefully in response.

"I will admit that I was upset when I saw you and Mason on my tv screen, at the Grammys of all places. Especially after not hearing from you at all besides that first text the morning after you spent the night."

I laughed quietly and looked away.

"Maybe upset is an understatement. I felt betrayed honestly."

I looked back at her. Her gorgeous eyes were rapidly filling with tears.

"These past few weeks I've been falling in love with you, but this showed me that you obviously haven't been falling with me. It blew my mind that you could form a connection with them so quickly. It makes me feel like I've imagined the past few weeks."

She opened her mouth to say something, but I gently put my finger to her lips.

"Please, let me finish," I said. "The way I feel for you isn't going to fade, it's not something that I'm going to be able to forget or move on from. I've lived for so long that you would think it's been forever. But what that has taught me is that the way I feel for you is a once in existence kind of feeling. I know with every fiber of my being that you are the one for me. So I'll do whatever it takes. I'll be patient. I'll be supportive. I'll be there for you no matter what. I'm in for whatever you are willing to give me. I'm holding out for the end... even if it decimates my heart."

Eva grabbed my hand, and pushed it against her heart, momentarily distracting me with my hand's sudden proximity to her perfect breasts.

"Is it my turn yet?" she asked with a small, sad smile.

I nodded, feeling a foreign emotion clogging my throat.

"I feel so much for you that it terrifies me," she started. "I can't explain what happened with Mason and Beckham. I can only say that it's almost like there are three parts of me that can only be filled by each of you. The connection I feel with you all takes my breath away. It feels irreplaceable. I've been alone and repressed for so long that with everything that's happened in the past few weeks, it's taking me a minute...and maybe a few panic attacks...for my head to catch up to my heart. I know I don't deserve you, but please don't think I ever meant to hurt you, or that I don't care."

My heart clenched a little. I noticed that she hadn't said she loved me back in her speech. But hopefully it would come. I didn't know much about her past besides the fact that she was an orphan who must have had a sheltered upbringing by her different reactions to things and her somewhat obliviousness to the attention that followed her wherever she went.

Mason had sent me a text last night that Eva had told Beckham some pretty messed up shit about what she had been through growing up. Hopefully with time, my love for her could heal her, and those broken, empty spaces inside of her could be put back together and fulfilled by just me.

We pulled into the parking lot of the stadium and Shelton started to drive towards the side entrance where the VIP guests could enter. I had the overwhelming urge to demand that he turn around and head back to Eva's dorm. Normally I enjoyed

Mason's concerts, and from time to time I would even join the band for some songs. However, knowing that every love song Mason sang, and every lustful glance he gave towards the crowd would be intended for Eva...not to mention all the energy he would be feeding off of Eva...was more than I felt like I could take.

I decided I was going to ask her if it was alright if I just dropped her off by herself. Maybe I could fake sickness or something. She probably didn't know that angels didn't get sick right? Just as I opened my mouth, she reached over, squeezed my hand, and flashed me a smile that took my breath away. I changed my mind in that moment about leaving. Seeing her with Mason would be torture, but her brand of torture was addictive.

I got out of the car and went around to open Eva's door before Shelton could get there. He laughed at me and I couldn't help but give him a grin in return. I knew I was a love-struck fool and I didn't care. Eva was bouncing slightly as she stood next to me. I assumed she was excited to see Mason, and again I couldn't help but feel a mix of jealousy mixed with despair rise up inside of me.

I had to choke it down so that I could return the sweet smile she gave me as we walked into the stadium entrance. Both feelings roared back when we got backstage, and Mason came jogging over. I took a step forward to rip Eva away from him when he had the nerve to kiss her in front of me. Shelton had come in with us and grabbed my arm just in time to prevent me from knocking him out. Mason pulled back and gave me a wink over Eva's shoulder as he finished hugging her. I was realizing that my best friend was a grade A asshole.

Eva at least had the decency to look embarrassed when Mason finally let her go. She was blushing and wouldn't look me in the eyes. I took her hand and pulled her further from Mason.

"We're excited to see you tonight," I told Mason, emphasizing the "we're" part of the sentence and hopefully getting it in his head that we were a couple.

Mason still had a stupid smirk on his face, and I had to take a deep breath and release it to get control of my annoyance. I had to keep reminding myself that Mason had to finish three more months of his tour while I got to see Eva everyday. That would give me enough time to solidify my bond with her, and for her feelings towards Mason to fade. That thought put a smile on my face and I was able to enjoy the atmosphere back stage as we walked to where the rest of the band was.

Eva waved to Lane who was already lighting up, as was his usual routine before the show. The guy was super talented, but a total head-case when it came to stage fright. Getting high was the only thing that seemed to calm him down enough to perform. Unfortunately he used it all the time now, and I couldn't remember when he wasn't high. Still he was a chill guy and a good member of the band.

We followed Mason to a side table that was full of food and drinks. Mason whispered something in Eva's ear, and she blushed again. I decided I needed a second away from Mason, and decided to go for a little walk.

I had just left the main room when a familiar face appeared. Courtney Rayne, Mason's ex-girlfriend, was lurking in the hallway, seeming to be gearing herself up to go see Mason. She was dressed about as provocative as I had seen her. She was wearing a black mini-skirt that was so short that I was pretty sure I could see the bottom of her ass poking out from underneath. She had on a corset top whose only functionality seemed to be to cover her nipples. Red lipstick and a wild ponytail completed her look. I smirked at her. Courtney was annoying as fuck, but tonight...tonight she was my favorite person.

"Hey Court," I said to her. She looked over at me and put

on what I guessed she thought was a seductive smile. I could see the underlying nervousness however. Courtney had always known that I didn't like her.

"Damon, so good to see you darling," she cooed, using the high pitched affected voice that had always made me feel sorry for Mason.

It actually sounded British, a fact made all the more annoying since I knew that Courtney Rayne, aka Twilla Smith, was born in a little town in Arkansas.

"Did you come to see Mason?" I asked innocently.

She began to play nervously with the bottom strands of her ponytail.

"You know me, just trying to be the supportive girlfriend before he leaves for Europe and I don't get to see him for awhile."

I raised my eyebrows in surprise. Was she that delusional that she would think Mason wouldn't have mentioned to me that he had broken up with her, or that I wouldn't have noticed that someone besides herself was on his arm at the Grammys? Hmmm, how to play this.

"I'm sure Mason will be excited to see you," I told her, waving her in.

I smirked to myself as she went in the room. I'm sure Eva wasn't aware that Mason had broken up with his girlfriend the night that he met her.

I gave the situation a few minutes, and then walked back into the room. The energy in the room was fraught with tension. Mason was gesturing angrily at Courtney who was in tears. Eva had walked over to Lane, watching Mason and Courtney out of the corner of her eye, distress written across her face. I was an asshole to ever give Eva pain, but I needed any advantage I could get on Mason and Beckham. Mason hadn't had an issue with throwing me under the bus by mentioning Selena. I didn't mind returning the favor.

Eva saw me and walked over to me quickly.

"Maybe we should go," she said worriedly.

"What's going on?" I asked, hating myself a little bit.

Eva's eyes got a little glossy.

"I think Mason has a girlfriend," she said sadly.

Before I could say anything the stage manager came running into the room.

"The crowd is going crazy. You've made them wait long enough. Any longer and I'm holding you in violation of your contract," he warned sternly, motioning the band to follow him.

Mason said something to Courtney and then started to walk our way.

"Mason, dude, come on," yelled Kevin, the band's manager.

Mason held up a finger and continued towards us, glaring at me the whole time. I was struggling to hide my smile, obviously not doing a great job of it since Mason looked ready to kill me.

"Eva, are you okay?" Mason asked questioningly.

"Let's just talk about this after the concert, ok?" she answered stiffly.

I was proud of my girl for having some backbone.

"Promise we will talk," he said. "It's not what you're thinking."

She nodded and Mason sighed, before kissing her cheek and walking after the band. I grabbed Eva's hand and gave it a kiss before leading her out to the side of the stage so we could watch the show. Annoyed as I was at Mason, the Riot was a damn good show and it was hard to pass up an opportunity to watch Mason perform.

I could tell Mason was out of sorts from the Courtney debacle as he strummed the first chords of his set. My mind momentarily went blank however as soon as the first notes of

Mason's melodic voice hit my ears. Incubi had various traits, but one that was the most envied was their gift of song. Within the few that held that gift, I had never heard anyone as extraordinary as Mason.

There was nothing that quite stirred up the array of feelings that incubi loved to feed off of better than singing. I had been listening to Mason's voice for thousands of years, and still was affected by it. In the past I would have been getting ready to grab one of the groupies, or several, and head off somewhere nearby so I could hear the music during my extracurricular activites for the night. Tonight, being so near to Eva, was almost more than I could take. I was so aroused that I was in pain. I couldn't take my eyes off of her.

Eva didn't seem to notice my frenzied state; she couldn't take her eyes off of Mason. She was glowing brighter than I had ever seen her, and her hair seemed to be slightly swirling around her head despite the fact that there wasn't a hint of breeze in the air. Mason has said she wasn't a succubus, but it seemed like she was gaining energy through the music. I didn't know what other creatures could do that. Mason started a song that she must have known because she started to sing softly under her breath.

Walking the halls at school today, I had heard many of the students gossiping about Mason's trip to Covet with Eva last weekend, and how they sang a duet together. I had heard it was an amazing experience for everyone who was lucky enough to hear it. However, my mind couldn't have comprehended just how amazing of an experience it really was.

Eva's voice was so beautiful that it tortured my soul. Whatever remnants of my heart that had still been longing for the paradise that I had lost so long ago, those remnants burned up, and finally left me in peace. My feelings for Eva seeped into every crack and cranny of my heart, until every inch was filled up with nothing but her.

Despite how soft she was singing, the unknown magic that she possessed must have been floating through the air because many of the people nearby were turning away from Mason to look at her. She sang on, oblivious to their stares, as was usual for Eva. Even Mason was sneaking glances at her. I could hear a waver in his voice as Eva distracted him.

I reached out to get Eva's attention when all of a sudden the light she was radiating grew even brighter. I could feel heat pulsing off of her. Mason looked over concerned and motioned for me to do something before people noticed that the light coming off of Eva wasn't caused by the bright stage lights.

Fifteen
Eva

"Sing me a song my darling," my sweet mother wheezed out. My mother, who was so powerful that the world kneeled at her command, could do nothing to rid herself of the plague that had been swiftly taking over her body for weeks. It had started as complaints of being tired, a symptom that had seemed to be soothed by afternoon naps and the healer's herbal tea concoction in the morning. While that kind of tiredness itself was unheard of from a being as powerful as my mother, in what seemed like the blink of an eye her symptoms had escalated until she was bedridden, so weak she needed to be spoon fed.

My gorgeous mother, a being possessing so much beauty that anyone who saw her was rendered momentarily speechless, had aged in a matter of weeks. We were immortal beings. We didn't age. But my mother's beautiful, golden hair was now liberally streaked with silver. Her perfect golden skin had turned a mottled grey color and was marred by spots, wrinkles crinkling around her eyes. I had to hide my tears frequently, not because I didn't think my mother was still beautiful, to me she would *always be the most gorgeous being I had ever seen, but because it was soul shattering to see the spirit that had left my mother.*

"Of course mother," I whispered, although I didn't know how I would be able to choke out any words to help ease her suffering. Mother had always said that the stars had burst into song at my birth, ensuring that I would always have the most stunning voice in the land. I had always loved to sing, but lately, when I needed it the most, my voice had been failing me. My grief was beginning to consume me.

I had heard her whispering to Brianag, her advisor and closest confident, that her connection to the land was fading more and more everyday. We were all born with a connection to the land, but only the Queen and her lineage could control it. What I hadn't mentioned to my mother was that my connection to the land was growing everyday. I could physically feel the agony that it was experiencing as the plague on the land grew at the same rate that my mother grew more and more ill. I had run crying to Beckham as soon as I was able to get away the first time I felt it. I hadn't explained what was happening, I had just soaked in his steady, loving comfort until I regained the strength to return to my mother's side.

I had begun vomiting frequently throughout the day. I could feel the earth's anguish not only for itself but also for the loss of its Queen. Despite how sick my mother was, she was still highly attuned to me and had begun watching me more closely when I came to visit her. I kept what was happening to me away from her, afraid that she would become sicker from being worried about me. I had been spending my nights in the library, trying to find something in our scrolls that would tell me what was happening. I had yet to find anything helpful.

Sixteen

Mason was talking to Damon in a low, terse tone. I knew he wanted me to go with him. Both men had seemed to agree to date me until I made a decision, but this would be the first real test of that agreement. Damon finally huffed out a "fine" to whatever Mason was saying, and walked quickly over to me.

"Mason's going to give you a ride back to your dorm alright?" he asked, looking like he was telling me that he was going to a funeral.

I walked over to him and kissed him on the cheek, hoping my eyes conveyed my gratefulness that he was letting me say goodbye to Mason privately. A kiss on the cheek wasn't good enough for him as he swept me into his arms, kissing me so passionately that I lost my breath. I faltered when he let me go, momentarily dazed from the breadth of his kiss. Damon looked very cocky as he waved goodbye and strode off. I sighed a little as I watched him go. That man's backside was delicious.

"You can stare at my ass as often as you want, but I would prefer if you would stop staring at Damon's," said Mason amusedly, coming up behind me and enfolding me in his arms.

I looked up at him and gave him a timid grin. Out of the three guys, Mason seemed to have the least problem with seeing me with the others. I turned in his arms.

"You were wonderful," I told him emphatically. "I could have listened to you forever."

"I actually fucking sucked tonight. I was so distracted knowing you were watching. And when you started singing... that was almost more than I could take. You should have been the one on the stage performing," he said, stroking my lips softly.

I immediately felt bad.

"I thought I was singing under my breath," I told him.

"I think I could hear your singing from almost anywhere," he said. "It speaks to something in my heart."

He brushed his lips against mine quickly.

"Want to get out of here?" he asked hopefully.

"What time do you leave?" I asked, feeling desolate at the thought of him going.

Whatever it was that was growing between us was so new, I wasn't sure if it would last for him while he was gone. Mason's eyes darkened.

"My flight to Munich leaves at midnight," he said mournfully.

I checked my phone, it was ten. We only had two hours. Mason took my hand, and led me out a door backstage to where a car was waiting. He kept my hand in his as we drove, softly stroking it with his thumb while he gazed out the window distractedly. I looked out the window surprised, we were back at my dorm. I turned to ask him what we were doing, but he was already out of the car, holding out his hand to help me get out.

Mason kept his head down as we walked into the dorm, nevertheless attracting eyes and whispers as we walked in. He held out a hand for my keys and I handed them to him, still confused what was going on. He opened the door and I followed him in, abruptly stopping as I gazed around my dorm room.

Twinkly lights were strewn all over the walls. A gauzy canopy covered the ceiling, and colorful pillows were strewn over a rug that was covering the floor. There were white candles lit around the room, their light casting a surreal glow on the scene.

"How did you...?" I started to say.

"Rockstar, remember?" he said, giving me a grin as I thought back to a similar moment that had occurred right before he swept me off to the Grammy's.

I suddenly smelled something spicy and delicious, and my stomach gave an embarrassing growl. Mason laughed at me, kissing the tip of my nose afterwards.

"Let's eat," he said. "I'm starving too."

He arranged pillows all around us to lean against and started serving out food from little white boxes.

"I ordered us food from my favorite Thai place in New York," he explained, pointing out what everything was.

I hadn't ever had Thai food, and I savored the first bite of it that I scooped into my mouth. Looking at Mason I blushed, he was watching me eat with a kind of dazed expression on his face.

"What?" I asked, wiping my face to make sure I didn't have noodles stuck somewhere.

"Nothing," he said. "I just didn't know that I could get a hard-on watching a girl eat."

I scoffed at him and tossed a noodle at him. He playfully caught it with his tongue and then it was my turn to get a little hot and bothered as he held my gaze as he somehow sexily sucked it into his mouth.

Continuing to eat, we chatted back and forth. Mason told me all about his favorite bands and famous musicians that he had met throughout time. He was talking about a dinner he had once had with the Beatles in their heyday when his phone beeped. He cast a glance at it and swore.

"What's wrong?" I asked, concerned with how pissed off he looked.

"Management wants to leave an hour early," he explained. "Something about avoiding a storm that is supposed to hit soon. Which means..." he looked at his watch. "I have to leave in just a few minutes now."

He looked at me.

"I don't want to have to leave you," he said seriously, taking both of my hands in his. "Promise me something," he said.

I nodded at him, so captivated by the love and longing I saw swirling in the dark blue depths of his eyes that I would have promised him almost anything.

"Don't forget about me?" he asked. "You're going to have a lot of time with Damon...and probably Beckham in the next few months while I'm gone. Don't let the space in your heart that I've managed to carve a place for myself be filled up by them."

I smiled gently at him.

"I wouldn't even know how to go about letting you out of my heart," I told him reassuringly.

He picked up a book that I hadn't noticed sitting behind him. He opened it up and showed it to me. The first page was a picture of Munich, Germany. It had showtimes listed, along with various phone numbers.

"This is my entire tour. It's where I will be at all times, when I'm performing, what numbers I can be reached at. I want you to call me anytime you want. Heaven knows I will want to talk to you whenever you will let me. I know you have a phone, will you FaceTime with me? I'll pay for the calls so you don't have to worry about that," he said hurriedly.

I was touched by the thought he had put into the binder. I nodded, and brushed a kiss against his lips. He groaned. The sound of it shot right through me, liquifying my insides.

"There's one more thing," he said nervously.

He turned a few pages until a picture of the Eiffel tower showed up.

"I checked your school schedule, and your fall break happens to fall over my Paris stop. If you wanted…" he took a deep breath. "If you wanted, I would really like for you to come see me. I'll take care of everything. I just know I can't go this whole tour without seeing you in person."

I was shocked…and absolutely delighted at the thought of walking the streets of Paris with Mason. I hadn't been anywhere, and had never even dreamed of being able to go out of the country.

I let out a little shriek and practically tackled Mason with my excitement.

"Is that a yes?" he said, laughing at my reaction.

"Of course!" I answered.

I stilled and stared into his stunning eyes again.

"I would visit you anywhere though Mason."

His eyes looked shiny, almost as if he was holding back tears. His phone beeped again and he looked away, trying to get his composure.

"I've got to go. But I love you so much Eva. I'll think about you every second I'm not with you."

He gave me an ardent kiss that left me weak at the knees.

"Don't walk me out," he said as I got up to follow him out. "I don't think I can actually leave if you do."

I stood up anyway and gave him a long hug.

"See you soon," I told him, giving him one more kiss.

He stopped for a moment at the door, his eyes roving over my face, seeming to be memorizing my every feature. He gave me a grin, and then walked out the door briskly, shutting the door behind him. I sat back down in the pillows, basking in his sweet words and the romantic little nest he had made for us. I couldn't wait to see him in Paris.

A few hours passed. I spent the time going back and forth between the binder he had made, and preparing for class the next day. My phone beeped. Mason had sent me a video. I clicked on it excitedly. In the video he was sitting on a stool in dim lighting, a guitar in his hand. He began to sing.

They say that only fools fall hard,
   They say you shouldn't show all of your cards,
   They say that love only leads to a slow death,
   But baby they haven't met you.
   They say that love makes men fall apart,
   They say that love is a poison dart,
   They say that love will take my last breath,
   But baby they haven't met you

You light up the room,
   I'm struck dumb at the sight of you,
   My whole life has been changed,

I used to be lust over love, now I've been struck from above,
   Baby, Thank God I've met you...

The song went on, each verse better than the one before. I played it over and over again, tears streaming down my face at this priceless gift. Mason's gravelly voice shot straight into my heart.

After I had listened to it probably a million times, I finally turned the song off and cuddled up in the pillows he had set up. I basked in the warmth of his love. It lingered in the room, despite his absence.

I wouldn't remember until later that I had never asked Mason about the Courtney girl who had shown up at the concert. I had been so distracted once he started singing, and then the surprise he had left for me in my dorm room. There was no way he had a girlfriend with how he had acted towards me…right?

Seventeen

It was finally game day. After Mason had left, I had enjoyed the rest of my first week of classes. Damon and I couldn't get enough of each other, and spent every second together that we weren't in separate classes or at practice. We hadn't talked any more about the fact that he was angel and what exactly that meant, but I was content for now to just continue to slowly get to know him. After all, we supposedly had forever to find out everything there was to know about one another.

I had continued avoiding difficult conversations with Mason as well. Although I had carved out time to Facetime with Mason every day, I hadn't asked about Courtney...or what exactly he was. Just as he had explained, the book he had made me had his exact schedule. He was so busy with interviews, promotional events, and performing though, that we didn't have much time to talk. He texted me throughout the day (and the night since we were so many hours apart) always letting me know I was on his mind. I hadn't asked what he was because I was a little afraid of the answer after the way Beckham had reacted. Plus, since we basically just had a texting relationship at the moment, I didn't think that the timing was right to try and have a serious conversation about either subject.

I hadn't heard from Beckham, and I tried not to be hurt by his silence. I'm sure his life was really busy. Still, I thought of the words he had spoken to me, and our moment on the beach, and couldn't help but feel upset that he obviously hadn't meant any of it. He wouldn't have let a week go by without reaching out to me if he really felt those things, right?

Damon had convinced me that I needed to spend the night with him in order for him to have a good game. Not that it was a hardship. I had discovered that I never slept better than in his arms...or Mason's...or probably Beckham's if we ever got to that point in our relationship...

Damon had already left to go have breakfast with the team when my phone alarm rang, signaling I needed to get ready to go to the stadium and meet up with the rest of the cheer squad.

I laid in bed for a second longer remembering how sweet Damon had been the night before. He had a mandatory team dinner he had to attend, but he had made sure that Shelton picked something up for me to eat. It had been waiting for me when I arrived at the penthouse. There were stacks of movies on the coffee table in front of the tv, along with an assortment of snacks like the first time I had come over. Over lunch this past week, we had made up a list of a hundred movies that I absolutely had to see to catch up with pop culture at least a little bit. I was pretty sure that all one hundred movies were laying on the coffee table for me to choose from. I had started one called Titanic, and was so engrossed in the film that I didn't even notice Damon get home. I yelped when he appeared beside me. Laughing, he scooped me up with an exuberant kiss, and sat me down on his lap.

"Good choice. Titanic is amazing," he told me, settling in

to watch the movie. "Does it sound super cheesy that I love coming home to you?"

I smiled brightly at him and gave him a kiss, pulling a blanket around us both and laying my head against his shoulder. Leaning against him, feeling him absentmindedly play with my hair, I began to heat up. My imagination began to run wild with what would happen if his hands stroked other parts of my body. I began to fidget a little, trying to unconsciously ease the pressure I was beginning to feel. Damon paused and cleared his throat.

"Baby, I don't think I can handle you moving around like that," he said in a gruff voice.

I could feel something growing hard against me. I tried to sit still but the pressure only increased.

Damon's hands slowly moved from playing with my hair... to stroking my arms...to grasping my hips. My shirt had ridden up a little, and of course he had found the tiny sliver of skin that was showing and was now lightly teasing it with his finger. Suddenly he grasped me tighter, one hand coming up to tilt my chin up to him. He molded his lips against mine. I pressed against his lips harder, still trying to somehow ease the pressure that was building up inside of me. I opened my mouth, and let his tongue in to taste me. I had been kissed a few times before my stay with the Anderson's. Awkward boys had stolen kisses here and there whenever they got the chance. I remembered them all being awful experiences. They usually had bad breath, or their tongues felt slimy when they tried to slip them in my mouth. But Damon's kissing...Damon's kissing felt like he had been practicing for thousands of years, which I guess he technically probably had. Every stroke of his tongue was masterful. My senses were in overload between his clean scent and his delicious taste.

I squirmed more, and he let out a groan, finally depositing

me next to him instead of on top of him. He grabbed one of the big sofa cushions, and placed it between us.

"This is my chastity pillow," he tried to joke, although the sexual frustration was very evident in his face. "I have to protect myself from all the sexiness you have going on."

I leaned back against the couch, trying to calm my breathing. Damon kept on sneaking looks over to me while we pretended to watch the movie, finally moving the pillow out of the way and pulling me closer to him. I had finally relaxed enough for the weird pressure inside of me to ease. As was becoming habit, I fell asleep halfway through the movie, cuddled up to Damon's side. I had woken up briefly when he picked me up and carried me to his room, laying me down in his enormous cloud-like bed. He had taken off his shirt and gotten in the bed with me. I had soon fallen back to sleep cuddled protectively in his arms.

I came back to reality when I saw a steaming cup of coffee from Leslie's laying on the counter along with a handwritten note from Damon saying that he missed me already, and couldn't wait to see me in my cheerleading outfit. Of course I blushed, despite the fact that he wasn't actually there saying it in person. I pocketed the note. Damon had made it a habit over the last week of leaving me sweet notes, and I had kept each one. After sipping the coffee, I dialed Shelton's phone number to see if he could give me a ride over to the stadium. He immediately replied he would be pulling up in the parking garage within five minutes, so I walked to the elevator to go downstairs.

Damon had lectured me about making sure I was only picked up in the parking garage because of the paparazzi that had been growing in numbers outside of Damon's building. Ever since video footage had been leaked of me singing at the club, and my appearance at the Grammy's had exploded on the news outlets, the press had gone crazy trying to catch a glimpse of Mason's mystery girl.

Somehow Damon and Mason's management team had kept my full name and location out of the press's hands, but Damon had become pretty paranoid, making sure we weren't ever photographed together and that we only did activities out of the public eye.

Shelton was already waiting for me when I stepped out of the elevator. He gave me a big smile as he opened up my door.

"How are you doll?" he asked, giving me a wink.

I had to admit that getting to see Shelton regularly definitely added to Damon's appeal. Shelton never failed to regale me with funny stories about Damon. We chatted about random things as he drove me to the stadium. I was full of nerves thinking about the game for both Damon and myself. Since Damon was so good, every major tv outlet would be at the game. I took a deep breath as we approached the stadium.

I could feel the energy in the air as Shelton navigated through the parking lot that was already full of tailgaters getting ready for the game. Damon had walked me through what to expect so that I wouldn't seem so out of place with not knowing anything. After thanking Shelton, I got out of the car, and walked into the varsity entrance where the cheerleaders' locker rooms were.

"Eva!" I heard Lexi call out.

She was hustling in from behind me.

"You are seriously the worst at answering your phone!" she cried. "I waited outside your dorm room for thirty minutes so that we could walk together, until I finally figured you had spent the night somewhere else!"

She suddenly got a mischievous look on her face.

"So...who was the lucky guy?" she asked.

I blushed.

"Damon asked me to spend the night last night," I said shyly, trying to make it seem like it wasn't a big deal.

"Ooh girl, you have to tell me how that gorgeous specimen is in bed. You're the closest I'm ever going to get to that."

I blushed even further.

"Ummm, we didn't sleep together...well we did sleep together...but we just slept."

Lexi grabbed her heart, acting like she was having a heart attack from the shock of my statement.

"Why the hell not?" she asked. "If I needed to cut off my right arm to get a chance with one of the "triplets" I would gladly do it," she said, only half joking it seemed.

I didn't say anything, just continued to walk down the hallway to the locker room.

"Are you trying to play hard to get?" she asked seriously. "Because a girl like you doesn't need to do that you know. I've seen the way Damon looks at you. I don't think he even remembers other girls exist."

I stopped outside the door leading to the locker room. I could share things with Lexi. That's what normal girls did with their friends right? And it's not like there was anything wrong with being a virgin or anything like that.

"I'm a virgin," I whispered, before opening the door and running inside without waiting to see what she had to say.

"Eva, wait," she called out after me.

Luckily, I had made it into the main part of the locker room where a lot of the girls from the team were already gathered. Some of the girls stared at me as I ran in, but they soon went back to getting ready when I didn't do anything interesting. Lexi popped up behind me, taking my arm and pulling me to the corner behind a row of lockers.

"How is that possible?" she asked.

"How is what possible?" I asked back, knowing exactly what she was talking about, but not wanting to answer.

"Eva, babe. You're the hottest girl I have ever seen in my life by far. The guys must be crawling up your door to get a chance with you. You're telling me that none of the man candy available ever caught your eye?"

I looked everywhere but at her.

"I didn't have a lot of chances to interact with boys," I answered uncomfortably.

"Okaaay..." she answered.

She softly touched my shoulder.

"Hey, I'm sorry. I'm being super in your business and you don't even know me well enough at all to feel comfortable sharing things like this. You don't have to feel uncomfortable with me about anything though. I already know we are going to be best friends."

Lexi gave me a big hug, and then finally took a step back, letting me have a little bit of personal space finally.

"Let's go get ready for the game," she squealed suddenly, her bubbly personality returning in full force, a definite 180 from the conversation we had just had. I smiled at her, glad that she was letting it go and not running from my social awkwardness. I shook off the conversation and did my best squealing impersonation back to her. Weirdo or not, this was my first college football game and nothing was going to dampen my mood.

Eighteen

Lexi primped me to within an inch of my life. My hair was in a high pony tail, and expertly curled into ringlets. She had lined my eyes with a dark black eyeliner and two coats of mascara, making my eyes pop like crazy since my eyelashes were so long and dark naturally. I had watched her put a million products on her face, layer after layer of makeup that I didn't think she needed. When I said so, Lexi explained to me that we had to wear heavier makeup during football games so that we would look better on camera.

"Lucky bitch, I can't even think of what to put on you," she said. "I don't think I could even see your pores if I got a microscope."

I powdered my nose and pretended not to hear her. Finally after an hour of getting ready, Selena called us together for a pregame meeting. She rattled on about making sure we didn't embarrass the team. After ten minutes of lecturing, Coach Ryan graciously stepped in, cutting Selena off mid-sentence and giving us a pep talk to try and counteract the threats that Selena had just leveraged against us. Then, it was time to go out to the underground tunnel that led up to the field.

Lexi had explained to me that we would run out onto the field before the football team, but I still felt butterflies as we waited for the team to come out. I watched as the football team started to stream out of the underground entrance to their locker room. The first couple of players almost tripped when they saw us standing in the hallway. I looked down at my uniform. Rothmore's school colors were red, black, and white. My uniform consisted of a black sports bra type top that had Rothmore in red and white across the front, and then a black mini skirt. I felt really uncomfortable showing this much skin, and the looks that the players were giving me as they came out in the tunnel made me even more self conscious. I didn't think it was possible to petition Coach to let me wear a t-shirt, so I would have to make the best of it I laughed to myself.

At that moment, Eric came out, making a beeline towards me as soon as he saw me. Right before he got to me one of the football coaches barked out his name, saving me. I was beginning to think that the coaches were actually guardian angels in disguise with how much they kept Eric away from me.

My jaw dropped when Damon stepped out into the tunnel. A lot of the girls started screaming when they saw him. He smiled at them and waved, and then turned towards me, giving me a smoldering look in the way that only Damon could. My heart leapt.

If I thought he looked good in everyday clothes, or even in his practice pads...nothing compared to him in his uniform. The Rothmore home uniforms were all black, and they left nothing to the imagination. He had turned to answer a question that someone on the team had asked him, and I found myself drooling over his butt. Damon Pierce was dangerous. Not that I had doubted his powers before, but this was on a whole other level. Damon walked over and wiped imaginary drool from my mouth, or it could have been real drool. I couldn't be blamed for my reaction to him at the moment.

"See something you like baby?" he asked with a smirk.

I nodded profusely, inwardly yelling at myself. There was no playing it cool with these boys. He leaned in close to me, the scruff on his face tickling my ear.

"You look so fucking hot baby. I'm dying to drag you off and start back where we left off last night."

I don't think I could have blushed any harder than I did at that moment. He pulled me in for a kiss in front of everyone, prompting most of his team to give a big cheer, and causing Coach Ryan to yell at us to "break it up."

At that moment, the horn sounded from up the tunnel. It was time to go out on the field. Adrenaline hit me as my feet touched the turf. Since we usually practiced on the fields next to the stadium, we had been practicing this last week in the stadium so that we could get our spots right for our game performance. Despite those practices, nothing could have prepared me for what this felt like. I had read that the Rothmore football stadium could hold 70,000 people, an architectural feat in New York City, but I hadn't really comprehended what that many people would actually feel like. There were people everywhere. The field was full of the marching band, reporters, medics, and tv camera crews.

We ran to the sideline to start cheering as the football team started to run out on the field. The noise of the crowd was deafening. A chant of "Damon, Damon" started, and I saw Damon waving at the crowd. I wondered if he had already taken the medicine he had told me about, and how long it lasted. He certainly still looked supernaturally perfect as he tossed the football to a teammate for warmup. I tried not to be distracted with how the muscles in his arms and hands flexed so sexily as he threw the ball.

"Eva!" Lexi whispered from next to me. "The camera is on you, try to smile!"

I immediately turned on my smile, mentally forcing myself not to stare at Damon anymore. The cameras were indeed facing right at me, and Coach Ryan was motioning at me from the sidelines to get a move on.

We started a new cheer that involved me doing a few complicated flips in front of the crowd. I got into position and began to execute the flips, the crowd in front of me going crazy. As I finished, I stumbled on my last step. I grabbed my head. It felt like a million hornets were buzzing in my ear. The buzzing rose in intensity. As it got louder I realized that the buzzing actually sounded more like a million voices talking at once. I shook my head, trying to clear it and get rid of whatever was happening. Someone pulled on my arm.

"Are you okay?" yelled Lexi.

Except I didn't think she was yelling, it actually looked like she was just whispering. What was happening to me?

I smiled weakly and shrugged my shoulders, motioning that I was alright. She looked at me suspiciously but went back to the cheer. I went along with the motions, pain continuing to pulse through my head from all of the noise. I looked over to where Damon was talking to his coach about 30 feet away from me. All of a sudden I could clearly hear their conversation.

"This is a hell of a team to start the season with, but I'm confident you'll pull us through," the football coach was saying.

I shook my head. There's no way that I should be able to hear their conversation from so far away. I stared at a couple who appeared to be arguing at least 40 feet away.

"I saw you staring at her ass Brian, you can't hide that from me," the lady yelled at the guilty looking man standing beside her.

What was happening to me? I experimented with people at various distances and learned that if I focused hard enough on the person, there was almost no distance in the stadium that was too far for me to hear what they were saying. I also learned that if I didn't focus on one person, the buzzing of all of the voices would return, practically paralyzing me in the process from how loud everything got.

There was an extremely quiet girl on the team named Diane. She was friendly with everyone, but didn't seem to like conversation very much. I focused on her for the rest of the pregame, which provided me some much-needed relief. I was so busy trying not to blast out my eardrums by focusing on Diane, that I didn't notice Damon surreptitiously trying to get my attention while pretending to grab a drink on a bench nearby until Lexi nudged my shoulder.

"Hey baby," he said, still pretending to be drinking his water and watching the crowd in an effort to throw reporters off that fact that we were together.

I couldn't help but laugh. Everyone was still looking over to where we were standing, they were always looking at me despite my best efforts to blend in.

"Having fun?" he asked me, his voice blaring out at me.

"There's something wrong with me I think," I told him hurriedly since the game was about to start. He looked at me sharply.

"What's wrong?" he asked.

"I can hear...everything," I told him, struggling to clearly explain what was happening to me.

His worried expression relaxed.

"Beckham thought something like this might happen," he said, pulling two small objects out of a bag on the bench next to him. "I've been keeping some ear plugs around just in case. They're a heavy-duty kind, and they should help keep the noise level down until you're able to learn how to manage it."

"Beckham's been expecting this?" I asked confused.

Damon was about to open his mouth when his coach blew his whistle, looking over at Damon disgruntledly.

"I'll explain everything later," he said. "Just put them in your ears for now so that you can get through the game comfortably."

I nodded and did as he said. I sighed in relief as the ear plugs settled into place. The roar of the crowd died down to a manageable level, and I could stop concentrating so hard on sweet Diane and resume normal conversations with Lexi and my other teammates.

With the ear plugs in, I returned to cheering. The energy in the stadium was crazy. People were absolutely out of their mind with excitement to see Damon play. Once the game started, I could see why. Damon Pierce was enthralling.

No matter what the other team did, Damon was better. Our defense seemed to be struggling today, and Mt. Whitmore College was marching down our field almost every time it seemed like. Damon didn't even seem phased. Our team scored every single time thanks to him. Whether he was running it in for a touchdown, or throwing it down the field for one, he was perfect every time. Examining him closely I could tell the difference between him without the magic pill, and him with the magic pill though. He was less polished, less fluid in his movements, less...angelic.

Watching Damon's face during the game I could see that he absolutely loved playing. I was happy that he had this in his life. Just like Mason's music, and Beckham's acting, playing football seemed to complete something in Damon.

At halftime we were up by two touchdowns. The team ran off the field to the locker rooms while we prepared to perform the halftime show. Getting into position, a roar from the crowd caught my eye. I thought I saw a familiar golden head walking along the sidelines. Was that Beckham?

Coach yelled at us to pay attention, and I turned my attention back to the crowd, waiting for the music to play that signaled the start of our routine. For some reason I had been put at the very front center of the formation for most of the routine, and my stomach fluttered with nerves about screwing up. The music began, and I began to move. The stiffness of my movements slowly faded away as I enjoyed the dance routine we were performing. I could feel the eyes of the crowd focused on me, even the reporters had turned their cameras towards our routine, but I ignored it all, lost in the music and my motions.

"Eva!" came a whisper from beside me as we ran to our groups that we would be doing lifts with.

"What?" I said, seeing that it was Lexi.

"You're glowing!" she told me frantically.

I looked down at my arm, and gulped...sure enough, there was a faint light emitting from my skin. I took a deep breath and tried to calm myself, watching the glow slightly fade with shocked eyes.

Lexi was giving me the side eye as we continued to perform. I knew I was going to have to avoid a lot of hard questions later on by the looks of things.

I focused on keeping my breathing and excitement under control so that my glow stayed muted. I would have to ask Damon about this little characteristic as well. I just hoped that I hadn't been caught on national television glowing...

Our routine finished with me being thrown up in the air where I was supposed to do a couple of flips. Adrenaline rushed through me as I soared into the sky, for a second it felt like I was almost flying. I executed my flips, adding in one more turn then was planned in the routine since I was so full of energy. The routine ended...and the crowd went wild. It seemed like we were almost getting the same amount of cheering as the football team did, and I looked around our squad with delight. Everyone was jumping up and down and high-fiving each other. I looked over at Coach and she had a very impressed look on her face as she gazed back at me. She gave me a thumbs-up.

We raced off the field towards the sidelines. As I got closer, I saw that the golden head I had seen earlier was in fact Beckham. I stopped suddenly, causing Lexi to curse behind me as she narrowly avoided running into me. He was as beautiful as I had remembered.

He was chatting with a couple of men standing next to him. The group was all dressed down, and seemed to be enjoying the view as they watched the cheerleading team run towards the sideline. He was wearing dark fitted jeans and a sky-blue t-shirt that was so tight you could see the barest outline of his abs beneath the fabric. I had to hold in my drool. Him and Damon on the field at the same time would probably cause some heart attacks today.

Despite the fact that he seemed to be occupied, I somehow knew that he was fully aware of where I was. I began to perform our sideline cheers, keeping one eye on Beckham at the same time. Various girls came up to the group frequently and seemed to be asking them all for autographs. While the rest of the group seemed very flirty, Beckham was simply polite, signing their papers and turning to watch the game which had just resumed.

Damon had winked at me when he came back on the field. I couldn't help but smile back at him. He didn't seem to have noticed that Beckham had come to the game. I wondered if he was as close to Beckham as he was to Mason.

The rest of the game flew by. Damon was absolutely amazing. Towards the end, I wondered if the medicine was wearing off as his play seemed to definitely border on otherworldly. Rothmore pulled off the win despite the crap performance of the defense, winning by 15 points.

Damon was so exuberant that he ran towards me after the clock ran off, picking me up and spinning me around much to the crowd's, and the camera's, delight.

"I made Coach turn on the tv so that I could see your half-time performance in the locker room," he told me before I could get a word in. "You were incredible," he told me with an awed look on his face.

"You were the one who was incredible," I said, loving the feel of his arms around me. He gave me a kiss and pulled away.

"I have to go talk to the press for a bit," he explained. "Wait for me after the game?"

I nodded my head and smiled as he jogged away, totally forgetting to mention that Beckham was here.

"What the hell is in your ear?" came a snide voice from the left of me.

Pain laced through my head as one of my ear plugs was yanked out, the roar of the crowd pulsing through my ear drums. Selena was examining the ear plug in her hand puzzled until Lexi came and snatched it away from her.

Lexi handed it back to me and I quickly put it back in, giving a slight sigh of relief as the overwhelming noise was muffled. Lexi began to open her mouth, presumably to tell Selena off, before another voice cut her off.

"Still putting your hands where they don't belong I see, Selena," said Beckham from behind me.

Selena looked embarrassed to have been caught being nasty by Beckham, immediately changing her face to one that I supposed she thought was alluring.

"Here to see Damon?" she cooed at Beckham. "I haven't seen you in what seems like forever. Not since that night..." she said.

Dread curled in my stomach. It seemed that all of the guys were intimately familiar with Selena, well maybe not Mason, he seemed to despise her.

I turned to walk away with Lexi, but Beckham had other ideas. He pulled me away from the crowd, ignoring whatever Selena was saying to him as we walked away. He didn't stop walking until we were back in the tunnel, and I was being pulled into a supply closet.

Suddenly Beckham's lips were devouring me. All the frustration from his radio silence faded away as I melted into lips that were so achingly recognizable to me, they were like my own. He pulled away gasping.

"Why didn't you reach out to me this week?" he asked mournfully.

"Reach out to you? I didn't know I was supposed to. Why didn't you contact me?" I asked, my voice rising at the end in annoyance.

"I was giving you space. I thought after everything that we discussed that you would need time to think and that you would reach out to me when you are ready. I finally couldn't stand not hearing from you and came out here," he responded.

"Oh...," I said, relief flooding my features at his explanation.

"So does that mean that you wanted me to call?" he said, a look of vulnerability shining through his eyes.

I nodded shyly and his face lit up. He was almost...glowing? Before I could mention anything he was kissing me again and everything around me faded. It seemed like it was hours before we emerged from the supply closet, both of us slightly rumpled from our passion. We walked out of the tunnel and stopped short. Damon and Lexi were waiting there, both wearing twin looks of annoyance.

"There you are!" called out Lexi, now looking relieved rather than annoyed. "Where have you been? I had to cover with Coach. Thank goodness you totally rocked that routine today, or she would have been fuming at you for disappearing!"

"It was my fault," said Beckham, flashing his trademark grin at her.

I couldn't help but laugh watching Lexi go sort of cross-eyed under the weight of Beckham's charm.

"Hey Beck," said Damon, sort of stiffly.

I watched Beckham let out a breath, seeming to be bracing himself for some sort of confrontation. But much to both of our surprises, Damon didn't say a word about me disappearing with Beckham. He simply clapped Beckham on the back with a grin and gave him the man hug that all of them were so fond of.

"The team will be celebrating tonight, and I'd really like for you to be there with me," he told me, his face bracing for disappointment.

"I was just going to ask if she could do dinner with me, and then I can bring her right back," interjected Beckham. He looked at me. "Would that be alright?"

I nodded eagerly, and then looked at Damon to make sure he wasn't upset. His face was hard to read.

"Call me when you're done?" he asked. "I can text you the address of the party."

He looked at Beckham.

"You're coming too since you're in town I assume?"

Damon's face clearly stated that he was just asking to be polite.

"I actually have some scripts to go over," said Beckham.

I couldn't help but feel sad that I wouldn't be able to be with both of them all evening. Beckham and I said our goodbyes to Damon and Lexi, Lexi promising to meet me at the party later on. Beckham took my hand excitedly and led me to a waiting town car.

Nineteen

I realized as we were walking that I was still in my uniform.

"Can we stop by my dorm so I can change?" I asked Beckham.

"You will want to keep that on. All the rest of the team will have them on at that party tonight," he explained as I stepped into the backseat of the car.

"Oh ok," I said, a little nervous at the thought of the party, and how many people were going to be there. I had about reached my limit for the day with how packed the stadium had been for the game.

Beckham must have noticed my unease.

"If you're not having fun, text me at any time and I'll pick you up angel," he said sweetly, wrapping his arm around me.

I laid my head on his shoulder, so happy to see him again. We chatted as we headed to dinner. Beckham wouldn't tell me where we were going, only that it was a surprise.

We pulled up in front of a high-rise. A doorman in a bright red uniform hurried over to the car to open our door. Beckham led me inside as the town car pulled away. I looked around in awe at the lobby of wherever we were. Everything was sleek and shiny...and very intimidating in its elegance.

Beckham led me into an elevator and I watched as the numbers slowly went up as the elevator moved. The doors opened, and I stepped out into a gorgeous apartment. From the enormity of the space, and how high the floor to ceiling windows rose, it looked like he had led me to a penthouse similar to Mason and Damon's.

"Where are we?" I asked, as I gaped at the lavish furnishings of blacks and greys around me.

"Home," he said simply, staring at me in amusement as I continued to gape and explore the space.

I looked at him quizzically.

"What do you mean?" I asked.

"I bought this place," he said, shrugging his shoulders. "I knew as soon as you left that I needed to be wherever you were. You just started school, so I came here. You can see me or not see me whenever you want," he explained hurriedly. "I just needed to be near you."

Beckham looked young and vulnerable, standing in front of me with his hands in his pocket, waiting for my response to his huge announcement.

"But what about your career?" I asked, moving towards him hesitantly. His face lit up.

"New York is actually a great place to make movies. I had a script I was thinking about taking even before I met you. You just gave me the nudge I needed. I start shooting on it next week."

With that obstacle removed, I ran the rest of the way towards him, jumping up and throwing my arms around his neck.

"Does this mean you're not mad that I'm stalking you, angel?" he asked, grinning.

"Stalk away," I told him, crushing my lips against his exuberantly.

More so than with the other two, it was easy for me to get carried away with Beckham. Everything we did just seemed so familiar that it didn't require any thought to slide into the next step with him. We had ended up on the couch, Beckham's shirt off, my hands sliding up and down his perfectly sculpted body, when the doorbell chimed.

We froze. I realized how far, and how fast, we had gone, and slowly sat up, smoothing out my hair.

"That will be dinner," said Beckham regretfully. I nodded, blushing as I observed his gorgeous body and realized that I had been all over him. He winked at me and went to get the door.

I started laughing hysterically when I heard a squeak and some bags crashing to the floor. I could just imagine what that poor delivery person had thought when the door opened, and a shirtless movie star appeared. We were probably lucky she hadn't fainted and was injured.

Beckham came back into view holding a few enormous bags. He looked chagrined and was blushing slightly.

"What is all of that?" I asked.

Beckham reddened further with embarrassment.

"I wasn't sure what you would want," he said, beginning to unload the bags while keeping his eyes averted from mine.

I watched in amazement as he opened boxes of sushi, tacos, barbecue, orange chicken and fried rice, burgers, pasta, and Thai food. I didn't even know where to start.

"Dig in," he said as began to put a little bit of everything on two plates. "One thing you should know about me is that I'm going to do whatever I can to make you happy. Even if that means ordering from ten different restaurants to make sure we eat something that you want."

I stilled his hand.

"One thing you should know about me is that I'm happy just being around you."

I gestured to the penthouse around us and the food.

"All of these things are amazing, but they are like frosting on a cake. The cake is what I'm really after, and that's you."

Beckham beamed, his face brightening. Looking closer I realized that it was literally lighting up. Like I had done earlier, his skin was actually glowing.

"Um, Beckham...you might want to look in the mirror," I told him hurriedly.

He looked at me puzzled, but stood up and walked over to a mirror on the wall.

"Oh!" he said, sounding shocked. "Well, this is unusual," he muttered, examining himself in the mirror.

"It happened to me earlier at the game," I told him. "It didn't go away until I started taking deep breaths and relaxing. What do you think it is?"

"Well I told you that Mason thinks we are something similar to each other, correct?"

"Yes?" I answered.

"This rarely happens to me. I can probably count it on one hand in thousands of years. I have to be supremely happy to light up for even a second. I guess it would make sense that it would be happening now, since I've never been as happy as I am with you," he said affectionately.

I thought for a moment. I had been supremely happy at the game today. Maybe that was it. Beckham looked over at me, his glow fading now that he was relaxing.

"Did you know you always seem to have a faint glow about you?" he asked me, studying me closely now.

I stared down at my skin.

"I do?" I asked.

"It caught me eye at the Grammy's. I was talking to

someone and I saw a glow from across the room. It was like you were a light flickering in the dark, drawing me in."

"You definitely have a way with words," I told him, hopping into his lap and giving him a kiss.

"I don't like how he looks at you," said Beckham, his voice oozing with frustration.

"He isn't looking at me that way," I answered, equally frustrated in having to have this conversation with Beckham again. "I have to deal with him since Mother is ill. That's all this is," I told him for what seemed like the millionth time.

"Let me at least come with you to the meeting," he implored. "The more Lord Tiberius sees us together, the less likely he will get any ideas about opportunities available to be king."

I didn't like this insecure side of Beckham. I sighed, and tried to see it from his point of view. I had never done anything that I could think of to purposely make him jealous. I hadn't even so much as admired someone else since I had met him as a child. Beckham was older than I was, and I had suffered through watching him in several relationships before I reached an age that he could take me seriously as actually being interested in him more than a child's crush.

I turned and touched his cheek softly.

"If I'm to be taken seriously, I must do this myself, my love. I can't imagine a world existing where you aren't waiting for me at the end of that aisle on our wedding day. Please support me by trusting me now."

Beckham signed and nodded reluctantly. I kissed him on the cheek succinctly, needing to hurry off to the meeting with my Father and Lord Tiberius. My mother had always told me "A queen is never late," but I didn't want to start off my first meeting in her role by being tardy.

Looking back at Beckham, I frowned. He looked troubled, as if he sensed something in the future that I was missing. I flashed him a smile and blew him a kiss as I walked away.

"Eva?" Beckham's voice pulled my from the vision.

"Sorry," I said, smiling ruefully, my mind going over the latest addition to the scene unfolding before me. "Just in la la land as usual," I joked.

For some reason I didn't want to share what I had been seeing with him yet. Not until I figured out what they meant, what Beckham was to me. A text sounded, Beckham frowned as he picked up his phone.

"Damon's wondering when he's going to get to see you, "he explained.

By the pursed look on his lips, Damon's comment was obviously a little more than that.

"I should probably go," I said.

As much as I was soaking up every second with Beckham after a week apart, a piece of my heart still wanted to be near Damon, especially to celebrate his performance that day.

Nodding reluctantly Beckham stood up and held out his hand, explaining that he would put the food away when he got back.

We got into the back of the town car, the driver whisking us away to where the party was being held. Beckham gripped my hand extra tight as we drove, obviously unhappy about the situation. How was I going to make sure that I balanced my time with each of the guys? I had already had to skip my call with Mason today due to the game and how busy I had been, something he was really upset about. I decided to think about that problem tomorrow and just enjoy the rest of the night. Hopefully it would be something that just evolved naturally.

Twenty

The air was a bit chilly as Beckham led me across a lush lawn, into a house on the "fraternity row" on campus. This was the football fraternity, Beckham had explained. Most of the after-football parties would be at this location unless Damon decided to throw one at his place.

Beckham didn't want to leave until we saw Damon.

"These parties can get a little crazy," he said. "I'll feel more comfortable when powers beyond making every person go crazy from wanting you come in," he teased.

I stuck my tongue at him, but inwardly braced myself. I could hear the music booming from inside. There were a couple of huge guys manning the door. Their eyes grew big as they saw us. One of them stumbled to open the door for me. The other tried to follow us before Beckham shot him a hard glare.

My eyes grew wide as we ventured in. Tommy's party seemed almost tame compared to this one. The air was a haze of cigarette smoke and booze. I was actually kind of surprised that Damon could handle it with how sensitive I assumed a supernatural's senses were after the disaster with my ears I had experienced today. There was a bar in the back room. Beckham got me a drink, watching closely as it was made to make sure nothing was slipped into it. Several large football players were stumbling around in a drunken haze. Others had several girls crawling all over them.

Beckham checked his phone and led me down the stairs into a large basement. Tables were set up in one of the rooms, and people were playing what I presumed was beer pong. A dance floor was in another room. The ground was slightly shaking as we walked into the crowd. I gasped as I saw there were actual strippers performing for the crowd on a stage set up in the far side of the room. Looking around, I wondered why Damon hadn't come up to meet us if he was so eager to have me at the party.

My eyes caught something and I saw red. Damon was having a heated exchange with Selena in a corner. She had changed out of her uniform into a tube top so small, it left absolutely nothing to the imagination. She still annoyingly looked pretty though.

Damon for his part, seemed nothing but annoyed as he told her something sharply. I was tempted to stay back and watch the scene play out, but I couldn't help but bolt forward when she tried to kiss him.

Sidling up to Damon, I slid in between them. Damon let out a sigh of relief, and wrapped his arms around me.

"As you can see, Eva's here. Run along now, Selena," he said, annoyed.

Selena looked furious to see me.

"Damon, I saw her with both of your friends. In fact today, she was slipping into a closet with Beckham. How does it make you feel that your girlfriend's fucking your two best friends?" she asked spitefully.

I reddened in spite of myself, her words hitting a little too close to home. How did he feel knowing that I was dating his two best friends? Guilt flooded me. This was never going to work.

"What Eva does or doesn't do is not your business. I trust her and that's all you need to know," he said.

Selena stared at us angrily. At that moment I felt sorry for her. If Damon, Mason, or Beckham ever decided they were done with me, I would be just like her, always trying to get their attention again. Selena was a terrible person, but she would probably be ruined from ever finding love in her life after she experienced Damon...and apparently Beckham.

I looked around for where Beckham was and saw that he was being mobbed by girls asking for autographs. He caught my eye and motioned that he was leaving.

"Are you okay?" he mouthed. After I nodded, he began to work his way out of the wandering hands. I watched as he finally slipped from the crowd, hustling back up the stairs, taking a piece of my heart with him.

Turning back towards Damon, who was watching me anxiously, I resolved to put all my thought towards my time with him. I couldn't control how this was all going to end, but I could give my all to each man during the time we did spend together.

Giving him a smile I asked, "So what do you usually do at these parties?" Damon looked relieved at my question.

"We pretend to be human," he said with an answering grin.

The rest of the night we did just that, and I loved every minute of it. Damon showed me how to play a version of beer pong that included paddles. We dominated the tables, winning game after game and hardly having to drink anything at all. Which was a good thing since I had discovered that I hated beer.

Lexi found me after an hour. She was sloshed and dragging some besotted football player with her everywhere she went.

"Eva!" she cried excitedly. "I've been looking for you everywhere," she said, grabbing me in a hug that almost knocked me over.

After playing a round of pong against her and her partner, we headed to the dance floor. Lexi was center stage, dancing her heart out, all over me and her partner. Damon stayed behind me as we watched her antics amusedly. I couldn't help but notice every time our bodies touched, or how his hands slid down my body. After what seemed like hours of him ramping me up, I was ready to go. We left after I promised Lexi a girl's night the next weekend, and that I would text her when I got back to my dorm.

Damon couldn't keep his hands off me as we walked to my dorm.

"Let me spend the night?" he implored as we got to my dorm. I nodded shyly, wondering how far we would go tonight after hours of foreplay.

I never found out, as Damon passed out on my bed while I was getting ready for bed. He looked so innocent and carefree in his sleep, the twinkling lights Mason had strung along the ceiling of my room casting a glow on his face. In that light it was easy to believe he was an angel. I smoothed the hair away from his face.

"Don't leave me!" he suddenly called out, obviously having a dream.

I laid carefully next to him, stroking his hair until he calmed. I quickly followed him into the best sleep I had experienced in a very long time.

Twenty-One

The next week passed in a blur. I felt like I would have been busy enough due to classes, homework, and cheerleading practice, but the guys also took a lot of my time.

Mason wanted to talk on Facetime every chance he could get, and I struggled to split my time between calls with him, and time split evenly between Beckham and Damon since they didn't seem fond of spending time together.

Beckham had started shooting his movie, and used the excuse that he only was off at night to wrestle most of my evenings away from Damon. When we weren't making out, he helped me begin to learn to adjust to my newly acquired sensitivity to sound.

Out of the three, Beckham was the only one who had gone through something similar, albeit at a much younger age, and so the guys had left it to him to teach me how to handle my new hearing abilities. After a week of training on how to filter sounds, I still had to wear my ear plugs, but my ability to manage the noise had greatly improved.

Damon's patience at not seeing me lasted until around

11:00pm most nights. He would then arrive at my dorm and either pick me up to spend the night with him at his penthouse, or he would spend the night in my dorm room. A big part of me wished that they would both spend the night, but I was confident that the guys were not ready for that by the pained expressions on their faces whenever one of them showed me affection in front of the other.

Lexi arrived at my dorm room at 7:00pm the following Friday, bustling with energy per usual. I smiled at her affectionately when I looked at the bags she was carrying with her. Of course, she had brought five billion outfits for us both to try on.

"Why do you always look so good?" she teased me, as she gave me a huge hug after dropping the bags haphazardly all over my floor.

She obviously didn't expect an answer as she immediately went over to the computer Damon had given me, and was fiddling around on it trying to find some music. I savored the feeling welling up inside of me at that moment. This is what I had always wanted, to just be a regular girl, with regular friends, doing things like getting ready together. Although calling Lexi regular was really selling her short.

So far there wasn't anything regular about her. In the short time I had known her she had proven herself to be a perfect friend. She was always there to stand up for me when Selena and her friends tried to attack me during practice, she brought me my favorite coffee from Leslie's when I had to work late during the week, she was always available to study or just hang out when I needed time away from the situations developing with the guys. In short, she was everything I had dreamed about in a best friend.

I laughed when she started to sing along to Taylor Swift. During our brief time together she had introduced me to all things Taylor Swift, and I loved it. I opened my mouth to start singing, but she quickly clamped her hand over my mouth.

"None of that now," she said laughing. "You don't want me to start liking you as more than a friend, do you? Because trust me, that first night at the club definitely had me thinking with my lady parts when you sang."

She started making kissy faces at me. I couldn't help but laugh, which embarrassingly turned into a snort.

"Did you just snort?" she asked with a shocked look on her face. "I'm pretty sure that's the first time I've seen you do anything that wasn't perfect," she squealed, and then raised her fists in the air. "I'm rubbing off on you. This is the sign of a true friendship," she yelled excitedly.

I threw a throw pillow at her from off my bed and rolled my eyes at her.

We spent the next hour fiddling with our hair, trying on outfits, and singing (or lip-synching in my case) to random songs on the "Girl's Night Out" playlist she had found. After trying on a few outfits which Lexi had promptly vetoed as "not sexy enough," I finally unearthed one top in the pile that I thought she would approve of. It was a navy blue off the shoulder bodysuit that was skintight and showed off every curve in my body. Paired with tight white skinny jeans, it looked sexy, while not being a huge departure from what I would gravitate towards normally. Lexi looked stunning in a strapless black dress, super tall black heels, and her strawberry blonde hair pulled back in a sleek pony tail. I went to grab some flats but she threw the ones I was trying to pick up in the trash before I could get to them.

"Hey!" I cried out, in mock outrage.

"There's no way that you are going to mess up an outfit like that with flats, babe!" she replied. "When are you going to get a clue how hot you are? If you've got it, you need to flaunt it," she said emphatically with her hands on her hips.

I begrudgingly slipped on the navy heels she handed me. She had curled my hair into bigger waves than my natural hair, before putting it into a half up half down style. She had also done a smoky eye on me with light pink lipstick. I was grateful for her help since I had yet to figure out most beauty things seeing as how I hadn't been able to even look at makeup for so many years. Mrs. Anderson's attempts to cut off my hair into chunks hadn't really encouraged me to try new styles with it either. Lexi roused me from the thoughts about my past that I would rather have avoided by tossing a silver clutch at me.

"Do I really need to bring a clutch?" I asked, whining a little bit now.

I actually loved to dress up, but it was fun to give Lexi a hard time.

"Shhh," she griped at me, grabbing my other hand and leading me to the door. "Let's start our night!"

Damon had offered to have Shelton drive us around for the night, but Lexi wouldn't hear of it.

"I don't want him having poor Shelton spy on us all night, and try to cock block us," she explained when I offered the ride.

Surprisingly, Lexi called *her* private driver to taxi us around for the night. I don't think I was ever going to get used to how well off all the people around me were.

"This is Max, Eva," she explained as a tall, buff man with almond skin, shiny black hair, and gorgeous brown eyes opened the door of an expensive looking black car for us.

He was dressed in a suit and hat and looked every bit the part of a driver that I had seen in some movies, if the driver happened to be a model. Max looked a little shell shocked as Lexi introduced me, so I simply smiled instead of shaking his hand, and quickly got in the car. Even though Max was gorgeous, I had all the admirers I wanted at the moment. Lexi smirked at me as she got in the car after me.

"I can't take you anywhere," she sang at me as Max walked around the front of the car to get in the driver's seat. I blushed. Lexi noticed everything.

"Where to tonight Lexi?" Max asked in a smooth, rich voice.

"Let's try Riot tonight," she told him. "Poor Eva almost got mobbed at Covet the other night, so we should probably stay away from there for awhile," she explained.

Max nodded and began driving away from the school. Lexi pulled a bottle of champagne out of a bin that was built into the back of the car that I hadn't noticed. There were two glasses attached to the bin, and she quickly and efficiently poured some of the champagne into both before handing me one.

"To a friendship to last the ages," she called out as she clinked her glass against mine.

I thought that was a sweet sentiment since we had only been friends for a few weeks. I felt so comfortable with her already, it was almost like we had been friends for far longer. We sipped our champagne, and gossiped back and forth about different things that had happened during cheerleading practice. I noticed that she seemed to be intentionally leaving out any talk of Damon, Mason, or Beckham. She mentioned how Lane had been calling her everyday, but she didn't go any further. I leaned back into the cool leather of the seats and listened to her chat about a hot guy she had met in her Chemistry class. She was getting to the part of the story where they had made out after class in one of the hall closets when Max pulled up to large warehouse looking building that had a line stretching around it.

"We're here!" Lexi cried excitedly, stopping in the middle of her story and downing the rest of her drink. I followed suit and waited for Max to get to our door to let us out.

"Do you want me to come inside?" Max offered to Lexi as she stepped out of the car.

"No, we'll be fine," she said, sounding amused at his question as she pulled me out of the car, and started towards the nondescript entrance of the building.

I eyed the building warily. Although there were a lot of people milling around, it didn't look anything like Covet had looked. It just looked like an abandoned warehouse with its shiny sheet metal looking roof and the colorful graffiti all over its walls. Lexi was still dragging me behind her as she marched up to the door.

A large bald man that towered over both of us was standing there dressed in all black, with a headpiece in his ear. The imposing looking man took one look up and down my body, and then moved aside to let us in. I smiled tremulously at him as I nervously followed Lexi into the dark entrance where I could hear the faint sound of music pulsing as I walked farther in. There was only a blacklight to light our way down the narrow corridor that was covered in neon graffiti, just like the outside.

We had been walking for so long in the corridor, that I was beginning to think that Lexi had brought me here to kill me, when we finally reached another door where another imposing looking man with an earpiece was standing. He too took one look at us and opened up the door next to him to let us through. A blast of humid air that smelled of fog and sweat hit me as I walked through the doorway. We turned one more corner, and found ourselves at the top of a metal balcony with stairs leading down to an enormous dance floor packed with people. The techno beats pulsed around me, and I saw that everyone looked like they had been streaked with the same neon graffiti paint covering everything else, creating an effect where everyone glowed under the black lights that were shining down on the floor.

It was a completely different feel from Covet and I instantly loved it.

Lexi squealed and waved to someone she saw by a bar off to the side of the room. She immediately started to once again drag me down the stairs. I struggled to keep up in the heels that I hadn't gotten used to walking in yet.

"Isn't this great?" she yelled back at me, dancing along to the beat that was playing as we walked.

"Yes it is!" I yelled back, trying to be heard over the music.

In truth I was very much out of my element. There was a strange feeling in the air, something that gave me an almost heady feeling, like I was actually sucking in pure energy when I breathed instead of the smoke that I saw swirling around me from the fog machines that were pulsing out particles every few minutes.

Lexi led me to the bar, and yelled out something to the bartender who looked at me with interest before turning around to grab whatever Lexi had asked him to get us.

"What did you order?" I asked, starting to relax a little now that we were mixed in with the crowd rather than staring down at them from the stairs.

"Their house shot," she said excitedly. "You're going to love it."

Someone on the other side of Lexi asked her something and she turned away from me for a moment to answer. While she was distracted I took the opportunity to people watch. I moved a little with the beat from the song the DJ was currently playing. I hadn't heard it before, which wasn't surprising since I still had a lot to catch up on from my time in the attic, but it was very catchy. As I people watched, I noticed that there was something strange about the people around me. They all were just a little too attractive. More like the guys, than normal people. I also saw that the air above the dance floor seemed to be almost sparkling.

I moved my eyes quickly away from some couples who were getting a little too close for my comfort, but I couldn't stop staring at most of the people I was seeing on the dance floor. A lot of them were unearthly beautiful in a unique way. Many had distinctive hair in colors that you usually didn't see like pale pink, or ice blue. I also noticed that many of them seemed to be almost glowing. I wondered if that was just because of the black lights and the reflection of the light off the paint that was streaked across many of them.

Lexi had turned back towards me and handed me a shot. The bartender was standing by; I suppose to see what I thought of it. I eyed it dubiously.

"What's in it?" I asked Lexi, and the bartender too by extension.

"A little of this, a little of that," he answered, smiling wickedly.

Lexi threw it back and I followed suit figuring if it didn't kill her, it wouldn't kill me. It was super sour, much more so than the other drinks I had tried, and I winced.

"Did you like it?" the bartender asked eagerly, obviously not able to read my face. I gave him two thumbs up while inwardly grimacing.

"Whoooo," called out Lexi, shaking her shoulders and obviously feeling whatever we had just drank.

"Let's go dance!" she cried, grabbing my hand and once again yanking me forward. I kind of felt like a rag doll tonight with all the tugging that was happening.

We walked through the throng of people, getting felt up and pushed against as we passed by. Like usual, the majority of the people stared at me as we passed by, something that I just needed to get used to. I could feel the strange energy even stronger in the crowd. I couldn't help but suck it in, feeling pleasure course through me as I did so. Lexi was watching me almost eagerly as I did so, and I blushed from her rapt attention. She laughed at my expression and started dancing. I followed suit, letting the distinctive melody guide my movements. I glanced around me as we moved, and soon became uneasy at what I was seeing.

There was a couple nearby embracing. I hoped it was my imagination, but the guy, a dangerously handsome blonde, was nuzzling her neck. I looked a little closer and saw a flash of what looked like a fang. The girl made a faint sound of gratification before seeming to fall closer into the man's body. My eyes widened, and I grabbed Lexi as I noticed similar couples doing the same thing all around us.

"What's wrong?" she said as I gripped her tightly.

"Are you not seeing this?" I whispered in her ear, gesturing with one hand.

"See what?" she asked confused before looking around and seeing what I was talking about. "Yeah...about that," she said, looking sheepish. "I may have taken us to a vampire club," she finally answered, searching my face intently to gauge what I thought of that.

My heart started hammering rapidly, and I could swear some of the couples started to look my way as if they could hear the sound. It was one thing to hear Mason and Beckham off handedly discussing supernatural creatures. I hadn't actually seen anything too out of the ordinary with them other then Damon's wings and the fact that they were gorgeous and seemed to be good at everything. But seeing actual vampires? And the fact that Lexi obviously knew about this supernatural world, and had decided to break me into it without telling me about it? That was all a bit too much. I nervously pulled her off the dance floor, deciding that we needed to leave right that minute.

Despite Lexi's reassurances that the club was perfectly safe, and that we should go back on the dance floor and try to have a good time, I decided now was a good time to try and fulfill my next idea of what a girl's night entailed by finding some good pizza to binge on rather than having *my blood* possibly binged on...

Lexi proved once again how good a friend she was by only complaining a little before linking her arm with mine and leading me towards a door near the back of the club. The door ended up being a fire exit, which led out to an alley. We began walking along the outside of the warehouse so that we didn't have to go back through the club to get to where Max was hopefully waiting for us. The warehouse was even bigger than I had thought, since it seemed to be taking forever to get around it.

"I really thought it wouldn't be a big deal," she said, wringing her hands as we walked. "I mean you hang out with basically the three most notorious supes in our world all the time. I thought that this would be nothing compared to that," she explained.

I just stared at her. I guess it was stupid of me, but I hadn't stopped to think what else was out there upon finding out that Beckham, Mason, Damon...and I guess me, were more than we appeared.

"Please tell me you at least knew about the guys," she said looking scared for the first time rather than just nervous.

"Well yes..." I answered. "But it's one thing to hear about it, and another to see freaking vampires. Wait... none of them are vampires right?" I asked, afraid to hear the answer. I still didn't know what Mason and Beckham were. Lexi looked less nervous now.

"I've never heard that they are vampires," she answered unhelpfully. "But it's kind of a mystery what exactly they are."

I had a million more questions to ask but decided to ask them once we got to the car. It was dark, not just because it was night, but because there oddly were only a few floodlights along the whole side of the building. It had been warm when we left my dorm room, but there was a chill in the air now, and my thin top wasn't providing very much warmth. I was sure that Lexi was even colder in her tiny dress.

The air seemed to get frostier as we walked along, and I pushed Lexi to walk faster as fear inexplicably crept up my spine. A shriek sounded right behind me, and I stumbled in shock at the sound. I turned around and let out my own scream when a black shadow...person...thing...stood right in front of my face. Strangely Lexi ran in front of me, muttering foreign words under her breath, blocking me from the advances of the shadow creature.

Whatever Lexi was doing didn't seem to be working as the shadow stretched out a black vaporous hand that passed through Lexi's shoulder, stopping right in front of me. I took a step back, desperate to get away from the ghostly hand. Lexi let out a hum of frustration and began to chant the strange words faster, with more urgency. Despite the fact that I had started backtracking faster, the black silhouette hadn't moved any further away. Another scream choked in my throat as the hand finally touched me.

A young girl with black hair done up in two long braids was walking along a bright white corridor carrying a tray laden with two goblets, and a vase filled with dark red wine. The leather soles of her shoes scuffed along the stone floor as she hurried forward.

"You there," came a rough gravelly voice from behind her.

The girl stopped, the wine sloshing from the top of the bottle and drenching the tray. She looked scared of whoever the voice was coming from. "Yes my lord?" she answered nervously.

"Where are you going with that wine?" he asked with a suspicious voice. The girl didn't want to answer. She was one of the Queen's handmaidens, and had been sent to fetch the wine for her. The girl was trying to hurry because she knew that Master Beckham would be slipping in to visit the Queen soon,

and she didn't want to disturb them. But this man could not find out about the Queen's secret. He had already done enough to destroy everything that made the Queen happy.

"I was just headed to the kitchen, my lord. One of the dignitaries just finished with their wine, and asked me to take this back for them. Is there anything I can help you with?" she asked, praying that he wouldn't look too closely at the tray since the vase was obviously full. The man said nothing, but made a shooing motion with his hand while still eyeing her suspiciously. The girl gave a sigh of relief and took a step forward, prepared to hurry away.

"Lara," the man said in the same growl, but this time with a triumphant undertone.

The girl stopped, beginning to shake with fear. He shouldn't have known her name. She turned around to face the man, sparks were starting to emit from his hands. She opened her mouth to scream...

I came back to reality laying on the cold gravel of the ground, with Lexi hovering frantically over me, patting me on the face, and yelling my name in a panic. She sat back with a sigh of relief when she saw that my eyes were opened.

"Are you all right?" she said, her voice trembling a bit.

"I think so," I replied, thinking back to what had happened. "What was that thing, and where did it go?" I asked, confused.

Lexi looked at me seriously, "That was a specter. I've never seen one behave like that."

"What exactly is a specter?" I asked.

"A specter is an echo from a supernatural who has met a violent end. I believe humans call them ghosts. Different names, same concept," she explained. "I've never seen one go after someone like that though," she said, sounding worried.

"Where did it go?" I asked.

"It disappeared when it touched you. It's like you absorbed it or something."

I shivered at the thought. I didn't want to have anything to do with that creature.

"And I just fainted when it touched me?" I asked Lexi, confused how I had ended up in the ground.

"I don't know what happened. You fell forward into me though and I was able to lay you on the ground," she explained. She stood up and brushed off her knees before reaching out a hand for me.

"We need to go," she said urgently. "I'm afraid more of them will appear."

I grabbed her hand and we hurried away, my mind whirling with questions.

Twenty-Two

We finally made it back to the car where Max had been parked waiting for us. As we approached the car, we saw that Max was surrounded by a group of girls who all looked to be flirting with him. Our faces must have shown that something had happened because he immediately excused himself and hurried over to open the car door for us.

"Everything okay ladies?" he asked warily.

"We need to get out of here," said Lexi tersely, all signs of her earlier flirtatious manner gone.

We didn't talk in the car on the way back to campus, both of us shaken from our encounter with the specter. Max drove us back to campus.

"Where am I dropping you off, ladies?" he asked.

"Eva's dorm is fine," said Lexi in the same clipped tone as before.

Max pulled up in front of my dorm, and Lexi and I got out. Before we could walk inside, Max pulled Lexi aside and started whispering urgently in her ear. She nodded and kissed him softly on the cheek before hurrying over to me, and pulling me by the arm in the direction of my dorm.

Once we got inside, Lexi started pacing frantically.

"We can't tell your guys about this," she finally said. "They will never let me hang out with you again."

I kind of agreed with her with how protective they tended to be.

"We don't have to tell anyone. But that means you're going to have to answer my million questions," I said.

She looked at me resigned and then walked over and sat next to me on the bed.

"Fire away," she said.

"First of all, how do you know about supernaturals?" Lexi fidgeted next to me.

"I know about them...because I am one," she said, grimacing and refusing to look at my face.

I sat there shocked. It couldn't be a coincidence that the four people I was closest to in my new life were not exactly normal.

"You're not a vampire right?" I asked, not sure what I would do if she said yes.

I had seen the hungry looks that the vampires in the club had been giving us, and I wasn't sure that I could deal with my best friend giving me those kinds of looks. Lexi giggled at the look on my face.

"No, I'm not a vampire," she answered. "I'm sort of...a witch."

"What does "sort of a witch" mean exactly?" I asked in an interested tone. Lexi sighed, settling next to me, her shoulder brushing against mine as she shifted her weight.

"Your majesty, the plague is getting worse. The Eastern region has reported that all of their crops have shriveled. The ground is covered in ash. There is panic everywhere."

I looked at my advisor and bodyguard. Alexina or "Lexi," had been by my side ever since I could remember. Her mother had been my mother's bodyguard and advisor for her entire reign. Lexi's family came from a long line of powerful witches that had served the crown for thousands of years. Lexi had never known anything other than these palace walls and service to my family. She was more than my servant though; she was my best friend. With the exception of Beckham, I trusted no one more than her.

"Have the seers come forward with anything?" I asked anxiously.

That flower dying in Mother's garden had been just the beginning. Within days, other portions of the land had begun to black and wither, a phenomenon unheard of in Tir Na Nog, especially considering my Mother was considered one of the strongest queens to ever rule.

"They haven't been able to see anything, your majesty. Mathias told me that all they can see is black fog when they try to see anything past your mother's death."

I choked back a sob. Mathias was the head seer of the palace. Earlier this week he had personally delivered the news to me that he had foreseen my mother's imminent death. That the ancient, hardened, seer had tears in his eyes when delivering the news was a testament to how loved my mother was. I had forbid him from mentioning the news to my mother. I'm sure she was well aware of what was happening to herself. I sent him back to the seer tower, begging him to try and see anything else.

Lexi's mother, Brianag, had been working round the clock, attempting to come up with some potion or spell to aid my mother. She believed that the plague upon the land was tied to my mother's illness, but I knew it wasn't. The power that had been seeping into my veins ever since my mother first became ill meant that our magic was still alive and well and passing on to the next heir as it always had since our people's creation. What-

ever was causing this pestilence upon the land, and likely my mother's illness, was something we had never encountered.

I stood at one of the windows in my room, contemplating my next steps. I could see the edge of the blackness in the distance, soon it would spread all throughout the palace lands. I felt weary, as if I were thousands of years old. If I didn't find a solution soon, there would be no choice but to accept Lord Tiberius's offer.

Lexi walked up next to me, staring out the window as well. She took my hand in hers and squeezed.

"Whatever may come, I will always be here for you, your majesty. There is no cost too great, no request too burdensome. You will always be able to depend on me."

I smiled, a tear streaming down my cheek at her loyalty, as I continued to stare at the black in the distance as it slowly crept towards the palace. It was coming.

Lexi was explaining all about witches as my dorm came back into my consciousness. I couldn't focus on anything she was saying as I absorbed what I had just seen. I felt...mournful, mournful over a land I had never seen, and a queen I had never met. I cut Lexi off.

"Is it alright if we talk about all of this tomorrow?" I asked hesitantly. "I'm not feeling well all of a sudden."

Lexi's eyes flashed with hurt. She obviously thought that I was making up an excuse to get away from her. I wasn't, I just needed a second to go over everything I had seen lately. My mind whirled with images, images of another life and another time.

Lexi gathered her things and rigidly said goodbye. I smiled at her reassuringly, giving her a big hug before she left my room, promising that I would call her to hang out after my shift was over the next night. Her face brightened at my promise, and she looked relieved as she left.

After getting ready for bed I sent a text to Damon and

Beckham, telling them that I was going to bed and needed some space tonight. My phone immediately began pinging with texts asking if I was alright. I turned off my phone, needing some peace and quiet to think.

I had been lying in bed for an hour, going over all of the scenes of a life that seemed so familiar to me, wondering what it all meant, when I heard a fluttering of wings outside of my window. I sighed and opened the window, moving aside so that Damon could step inside. I expected a million questions about the night, and settled into my bed resigned to the fact that I was going to be exhausted for my shift the next day. Damon surprised me though, climbing into bed with me and holding me close. My door opened, causing me to jump since I had locked it. I relaxed back into Damon's arms when I saw that it was Beckham.

Beckham stood there awkwardly for a moment.

"Fuck it," he muttered, taking his belt off and pulling his pants off so he was just in his boxers.

"Damn it," said Damon, moving to the other side of me to make room for Beckham.

I was awkward at first as Beckham slid in to my bed. I guess I was lucky that Damon had ordered a new queen bed to be installed in my room after the first night he had been forced to cuddle next to me in the twin bed that my room had come with. The queen bed felt tiny with all three of us in it though, especially considering Beckham and Damon were both extremely large men. I rolled onto my side, facing Damon and allowing Beckham to cuddle me from behind. I soaked in their warmth and love, ignoring the fact that they were both hard as a rock.

Weighed down by my latest vision, I began to cry silently into Damon's shoulder. Neither of them said a word, simply offering soundless comfort to me as the night wore on. I fell asleep, the feeling of protection and love finally pushing out my troubled thoughts.

Twenty-Three
Beckham

I woke up in the arms of an angel. Literally. Eva had snuck out of bed, and Damon had snuggled up to my side with his arm stretched out on top of me. Eva was giggling at the foot of the bed, snapping photographs of us on her phone, I'm sure to send to Mason and Lexi later on.

"Eva," groaned Damon sexually as his hand started moving towards my pec as if he was going to squeeze it like he would a woman's breast. Terrified, I pushed him off the side of the bed.

"What the fuck!" yelled Damon, as he hit the ground hard.

Eva was now bent over from laughing so hard. I flew out of bed and scooped Eva into my arms, tossing her lightly back on the bed and stretching my body over hers. Eva's mouth was open in shock, none of us had really shown her our supernatural speed yet.

Damon was still sitting on the floor confused.

"I hate to break up the love fest this morning, but would someone mind telling me why I was pushed on the floor just a second ago?" he asked, the sarcasm in his voice apparent.

Eva grinned at me and I moved off of her. She pulled up the pictures on her phone and triumphantly showed Damon the one she had taken where he was about to fondle my chest. Damon shook his head in disbelief, flushing a dark red color. I had never seen him do that before and it sent both Eva and I into a rush of hysterics.

I had always been the outlier of the group. Damon and Mason had known each other for centuries before I came into the picture, and although I considered them my brothers, I had never bonded with them the way they had bonded with each other. It was nice to see Damon laugh in my presence though, since I knew he was furious about my attempts to date Eva. Damon stood up and stalked towards Eva.

"Don't pretend you aren't going to use those pictures for private time later, Eva," he said to her slyly.

Now it was Eva's turn to blush. I knew our little virgin wasn't having any "private" time, not that it didn't turn me on ferociously to think of her having some. Despite Damon's presence, I felt myself growing hard at the thought. Eva looked so amazingly beautiful sitting in her bed, her hair sexily mussed, and a flush still on her cheeks. Last night had been my first time getting to spend the night with her, and despite Damon's less than ideal presence, I had savored every second of holding her soft body in my arms.

Damon picked up his phone and swore.

"I've got weights and then team meetings in ten minutes because of our bye week," he told Eva regretfully. "You work tonight right? Let me know when you're going home, and I'll come get you. Then, we're going to talk about last night."

He kissed her lips softly, and a small ball of fury welled up inside of me at the sight of his lips on something that was mine. I shook it off, and averted my eyes when he deepened it. He then swiftly walked out of the room without saying anything to me. Typical asshole Damon.

I turned to look at Eva. She was looking after Damon, her eyes soft with love. I could tell she was already missing him. My stomach began acting up again. The more time I spent with Eva, the more I felt like she was mine, that she had always been mine.

Sometimes in my dreams, images would flutter through my mind, so clear that they seemed like memories more than anything else. I was always with Eva in them. Kissing Eva, loving Eva, wanting Eva. It was a bitter pill to swallow that Eva haunted my every moment, waking and asleep, yet I didn't occupy all of hers. I almost didn't want my dreams to be memories of something we had both forgotten. What could be worse than knowing that I had once been her everything, and that somehow I had lost her?

Eva turned towards me and smiled. I hadn't forgotten that something had happened last night while she was out with Lexi. I had learned though that Eva wasn't a big sharer. She would clam up if you tried to push her into telling you something. She had to tell me on her own time even if it drove me crazy from not knowing what was bothering her.

What happened last night was just one of the things I was waiting for her to talk to me about. The other, was where she kept disappearing to around me. She would often go into a trance, not responding despite my repeated attempts to rouse her. When she would come out of it she would try to play it off like it was nothing, but I had noticed she would get really quiet afterwards, like she was studying something in her mind.

I hadn't been crazy about Eva going to a club without one of us. Anyone who met her basically became her stalker, and I wasn't sure that Lexi was up to the task of protecting her. I tried to temper back my overprotectiveness though. That was Damon's job to be the arrogant, overprotective bastard. If he wasn't careful, it would eventually push Eva away. Wouldn't that be nice...

Lexi was a conundrum to me. I didn't know if the other guys noticed, but she was always popping around no matter what we were doing. Of course, she always had a perfectly reasonable explanation for why she was there too, but it still seemed suspicious. I got that she wanted to be best friends with Eva, but there was something about her that rubbed me wrong. Like everything she was doing wasn't as it seemed.

"Beckham?" Eva said, her voice bringing me out of my reverie. She was looking at me inquiringly. I grinned reassuringly at her.

"Want to get breakfast with me? And then I thought we could catch a movie before your shift?" I asked her hopefully. It wasn't often that Damon was busy, and I could be ensured that he wouldn't interrupt us. I was grateful that Mason was held up on his tour. I knew he was probably dying right now, literally and figuratively, without being able to see her in person. I was still quizzical how he was going to go so long without feeding on anything but the emotions generated during his concerts. I was pretty sure he had been having some sort of sexual activity every day before he met Eva.

"Can we go see your new movie?" she asked hopefully. I groaned. I hated watching myself in movies. And trying to gauge if she was liking it the whole time would be miserable.

"I saw Beyond Eden. You were breathtaking in it," she told me, her eyes lighting up as she described her favorite parts. Suddenly her seeing as many movies of mine as possible didn't seem like such a bad idea. Damon and Mason had both been able to impress her with their skills, I needed to start trying to impress her with mine.

As was her new habit according to Damon, Eva got dressed in her closet. I hated to break it to her, but it got me hot just thinking about her changing clothes in the same room as me, even if I couldn't see anything. Eva emerged from the closet, looking amazing as usual in tight black skinny jeans, and an off the shoulder black top. She applied some red lipstick in a mirror and I struggled to hide my reaction. Visions of those lips wrapped around my cock surged into my head and I had to start thinking of movie quotes to calm myself down.

Unaware of my thoughts, Eva put her arm in mine. I grabbed a baseball cap to try and disguise myself until we could make it to the car waiting out front. This was going to be an incredible day.

Twenty-Four
Eva

My shift at Moxie had run very, very late. The restaurant seemed to grow in popularity every week, and Derek and I had been running all over trying to keep our tables happy. The guys had been trying to get me to quit my job, but I loved the independence the money I made from it gave me. I had been able to start saving up a nice little nest egg. Derek had become a pretty good friend as well, and I enjoyed hanging out with him during my shifts.

I probably should have called Damon like he had requested, but the cool night air felt good on my face compared to the stifling heat of the restaurant, and I liked pushing back at his bossiness sometimes. I walked along the sidewalk, thinking about nothing in particular, savoring the sounds of the city as usual. I would never take New York City and her beauty for granted.

The streets were quieter than usual, the ever-present crowd dwindled in presence due to the late hour. My thoughts turned to my glorious day with Beckham. His new movie had been even better than the other one, and I loved seeing the light flush to his cheeks when I praised his work.

I heard rustling behind me, catching my attention and making me look behind me to see if anyone was there. I didn't see anything. Nevertheless, I quickened my pace, the ease of my walk faltering. There was one spot in my walk that I always hated, where I had to go down a narrower alley, and it was coming up. I was tempted to try and stop and get a cab, but I hadn't seen one pass my route tonight, and I would rather get home quicker than waiting around for one. I took my ear plugs out of my ears, hopeful that my newly acquired sense of sound would come in handy if anyone was actually following me.

Furthering my resolve to make it home on my own, I hurried my steps even more, determined to make it through the upcoming alley at a breakneck pace. I made it to the end of the alley, relieved to see the streetlights in front me signaling I was close to the college. I stepped past the wall into the street, when suddenly a coarse bag was forced over my head, making me fall forward onto my hands and knees on the sidewalk. I struggled as rough hands grabbed me harshly by the arms, pulling me up off the ground, and attempting to pull me forward. I began to struggle, attempting to scream, but I was sure the bag was preventing any sound from getting out.

A cord was tied around my wrists, the cord digging and ripping my skin as I struggled. I was dragged, kicking and screaming the whole way. I was thrown into an enclosure, realizing it was some kind of vehicle when I heard the engine start up. I panicked even more and began to throw myself around the cabin of the vehicle, desperately trying to garner some attention from outside. Something solid hit me in my temple hard. Everything immediately went black.

I groggily opened my eyes and immediately began to struggle again, only this time I could move even less since someone had sat me on a chair and tied my legs and arms to it so I couldn't move. My head was pounding from where I was hit, and there was an ache in my left shoulder. I was in a dimly lit room in what looked like someone's basement. There was a single light bulb in the center of the room, and I could see wood stairs in the corner of the room leading upwards. As I continued to look at my surroundings, my horror grew.

There was a block of metal in the ground with what looked like chains attached to it. There was a dingy twin mattress beside it, with a faded quilt folded up at the foot of it. In another corner, there was a temporary toilet. I recognized it only because Mrs. Anderson had been a fanatic about food storage and emergency preparedness, so she had owned a few. I knew they had contemplated putting one of those temporary toilets in the attic so they wouldn't have to let me out at all. Mr. Anderson had convinced his wife that it wasn't a good idea, I'm sure so he could continue to fondle me when he let me out of the attic to use the restroom.

Shaking my head at this unhelpful train of thought, I examined the room again looking for anything else. None of the room items were a good sign. I had read enough books to know that situations like this meant that the kidnapper had prepared to hold you for the long haul. My throat started to close up as panic overtook me. Stupidly the first thought I had was about missing class. I loved my classes and everything about college, and who knew how long it would be before I was let go or I escaped, if I ever escaped at all. I began to rock back and forth futilely until the chair tipped over. I hit my head again on the floor as the chair crashed on the hard concrete. My head was spinning. The combination of the hit from earlier, and now the knock on the concrete, meant that I had to have a concussion. I wretched from the pain in my head, the vomit splattering all over my hair, face, and clothes. I sobbed involuntarily.

How had I gone from having everything I could want, to this? I tried to listen to see if I could hear anything, but my ears had begun ringing too much from my head trauma to make anything out. I stopped struggling, and just laid there continuing to weep. The basement was cold. Combined with the concrete floor and my injury, I had begun shivering uncontrollably.

My 18th birthday had been five days from when I was kidnapped. I wasn't sure how long I had been passed out, so I didn't know how close my birthday was now. I wondered if any amazing powers would appear like the guys had thought would happen. I mean escaping would be a nice present too, I laughed to myself. I bet the boys had planned something big for my birthday. I began to daydream what they had planned, while the cold continued to seep into my bones. Hours passed, my vomit from earlier had congealed and I could feel that my hair was now in clumps. I couldn't believe that no one had come for me yet. My mind imagined scenarios where I had actually been left somewhere alone for good, doomed to die alone in this basement of starvation or thirst. I eventually cried myself to sleep, overwhelmed with tiredness from my head injury and from crying so much.

I awoke when I felt a wet washcloth sliding across my face, softly cleaning up the vomit from before. My head still ached, and my eyes had trouble focusing. The confusion of being woken up by touch stayed as I realized who was in front of me cleaning me up. It was Anna Darcy, the Reverend's wife.

"Mrs. Darcy?" I inquired stupidly.

She refused to look at me, keeping her eyes focused on the task of cleaning me up. I was still tied to the chair so I began to rock back and forth again on the floor where I had fallen, trying to get her to look at me.

"You have to help me. I've been kidnapped. Please help me!" I cried to her.

Suddenly she clasped a hand over my mouth.

"Be quiet, you stupid girl. You don't want him to come down here."

I still didn't understand what was going on.

"Please!" I begged her. "Please go get Reverend Darcy. Surely he will help?"

She stopped trying to clean me up, and looked at me with a sad expression filled with pity.

"Who exactly do you think brought you here Eva?" she asked softly.

Suddenly understanding the situation, I wretched again, nothing really coming up this time but stomach bile, as I hadn't eaten in probably a day. I remembered his frequent visits to the house after the fateful lunch when I had found my acceptance letter, and the frustration and desperation he seemed to have on the night I had escaped. I had been so preoccupied with trying to escape that I hadn't put much thought into his visits besides thinking they were strange.

The sick feeling of dread in my stomach increased. I wondered if the Anderson's had a role in this. I was such an idiot. I had been so caught up in the excitement of the world that the boys were offering me, I had totally forgotten to take into account the publicity I had been getting. Of course, someone from my past was going to find me. Why in the world had I thought that the Andersons and the Reverend wouldn't get wind of where I was just because they lived in a small town? There had been pictures of me everywhere after the media got wind that Mason or Damon (they didn't know about Beckham yet) might be dating me. I stopped struggling and laid my head down on the concrete, feeling defeated. Anna must have been satisfied with the job she had done wiping off my face, because she stood up and dusted herself off.

"Do you want to stay on the ground or do you want me to help pull the chair up?" she asked.

"Just leave me here," I responded despondently. I'm sure anger would come eventually, but right now all I was feeling was fear and hopelessness. I didn't know how I was going to find my way out of this one.

"Reverend Darcy is finishing a sermon, and will be down later," she said, weirdly referring to her husband by his church title. "This will go better for you if you try and cooperate," she said stiffly, like she was trying to convince herself as well as me.

I closed my eyes, and decided to ignore her. I could feel the weight of her stare on me for a moment more before I heard her walk away, the creak of the stairs signaling she had left the room. She further ensured I would hate her for the rest of my life when she flipped the light switch, the room immediately going pitch black.

Twenty-Five

The hours seemed to last forever as I laid there feeling sorry for myself. At this point I felt truly disgusting. Anna may have wiped the vomit off my face, but I had needed to use the restroom hours ago, and thus had wet myself at some point. All of a sudden I felt the temperature drop even more. I groaned. Now was not the time for the "specters" to appear. An icy cold finger trailed down my face. I couldn't see the black shadow due to the gloom of the basement, but I could sense its presence.

"I obviously can't help you right now," I said angrily, immediately wincing from the pain still in my head. I waited for a vision to appear. This one took a while as the shadow continued to stroke my face with its icy fingertip. "I'm already freaking cold enough without you touching me," I yelled out.

"Oh dear," the old woman muttered to herself as she prepared the Princess's morning tea. "I need to start thinking of her as the Queen," she admonished herself. After all, if the rumors were true, the crown would pass any day now as the Queen's health continued to decline. The woman mourned the Queen already. She had always been exceptionally kind to the

woman, finding her a place in the kitchens as a young orphaned child, despite the fact that she was a human, and would only have a limited time when she would be useful to the palace.

The woman had spent her whole life in the palace walls. Her status as human meant that she was frequently ignored by the other residents. This meant that she often saw things that she shouldn't be seeing. Like the King dallying with one of the maids while the Queen lay dying in her chambers. Or how that Lord Tiberius fellow was always watching the Princess. She had seen him stalking her in the shadows, the Princess blissfully unaware as she laughed with that beau of hers. The woman could understand him watching the Princess in those times, after all the Princess was the most beautiful being in the realm, but Lord Tiberius was also always watching the Princess as she mourned the Queen. It was those moments that had worried the woman the most. After forty years around the palace, she still didn't understand why the creatures who lived here acted as they did. The malicious smile the Lord displayed when the Princess was sorrowful didn't seem right though.

"There's monsters lurking underneath that handsome face, mark my words," the woman muttered to herself as she finished making the tea, and began to trudge towards the Queen's chambers to see if she could cajole her into drinking some of it.

Walking through a back passage she had discovered after a few years in the palace, the woman decided that she would say something to the Princess next time she saw her. "She'll know what to do about such a thing," the woman told herself.

She had just turned a corner and was passing one of the many dusty rooms that lay empty in this long-abandoned passageway, when she heard a grunt from nearby. She noticed that one of the doors to the rooms was partly closed. Walking as silently as an elderly woman with a bum leg could, she approached the door, peeking into the room.

She couldn't help but let out a small gasp at what she saw. A being in a black cloak was bent over one of the maidservants, the poor girl's eyes were staring out lifelessly as she lay strewn on the floor. The cloaked creature had a long, sharp, ebony knife in his gloved hand, and was making a deep cut into the girl's arm. The blood was dripping into a bowl on the ground. The woman's stomach rolled, the bowl was already half-filled.

"I have to go tell someone," the woman thought to herself, panicking at the task. She began to back away as softly as she could when the hooded creature began to sniff the air.

"Little human...I know you're out there. Come out, come out, wherever you are," the familiar voice taunted.

The woman couldn't believe the cloaked monster was him. She turned to run, but a strong hand caught her arm before she could take two steps. The monster inhaled her scent deeply, before dragging her into the room she had just been peering into, this time closing the door behind them.

He threw her beside the maidservant, some of the sticky blood from the bowl, splattering her as she hit it.

"You'll be the perfect final ingredient," he said, as she struggled to sit up.

"I should have told the Princess," was the woman's last thought, before the ebony knife came slashing down on her.

I came back from the vision shaking from its gruesomeness, the light from the basement had clicked on, and I squinted my eyes from the sudden brightness after being in the dark for so long. When my eyes finally adjusted, I couldn't help but start to shake. Reverend Darcy was standing at the foot of the stairs, staring at me with a terrifying, manic glint in his eyes. The specter from before was nowhere to be found.

Reverend Darcy had lost weight. He no longer resembled the man I had first met at that lunch at the Anderson's a few months ago. He skin was sallow and grey tinted, like he hadn't eaten or seen the sun in years. He walked towards me, and knelt down in front of me. His eyes were bright and feverish, flicking all over me with some kind of sick hunger that shriveled my stomach.

"Eva," he said reverently, starting to softly stroke the side of my cheek.

I jerked my cheek away.

"Reverend, what exactly is going on?" I asked, knowing inside that I didn't want to hear the answer.

"Kylan, call me Kylan, Eva. We're going to be getting to know each other really well. I searched for you for weeks you know, and when I found you, I started to watch you. I saw you Eva. I saw how all of those men were taking advantage of you. I know you didn't actually want that, and they were forcing you to do what they said. But you don't have to worry about that anymore. I'm going to take care of you," he said, in the same abnormal voice.

"You seem to be failing in that regard," I told him saucily, gathering courage from somewhere inside of me, and gesturing with my head to where I laid still tied to the fallen chair, soaked in piss and vomit. An irritated look flashed briefly on his face before he took a breath and relaxed again.

"It is unfortunate that you have had to be in these conditions for so long, but Anna said she tried to help you and you tried to attack her."

My anger at Anna increased tenfold with the news that not only had she refused to help me earlier, but then she had lied to make my situation worse. I had never done anything to her to deserve her hate.

"If I untie you, will you cooperate?" the Reverend asked me.

At this point I was willing to not try anything if it included me getting some water and being able to get cleaned up. I nodded my head. He seemed to approve of this and pulled out a pocket knife from his back pocket, and started to saw at the ropes binding my arms and legs. I collapsed in a heap when the ropes were finally cut, my limbs numb from being constrained for so long. The Reverend gathered my wrists in his hands, and started to massage them. I wanted to throw up again, or at least yank my hands away, but I couldn't move them quite yet. He didn't seem to mind the fact that I was soaked in pee and vomit. He continued to massage my wrists with one hand, while he tucked my hair behind my ears with another. I shuddered and refused to look at him.

Sensing that I wasn't going to talk to him, he finally stood up, and then bent down to pick me up. His arousal was obvious as he slid me up his body. I couldn't see how he could even be attracted to me in my current state. I began to tear up again. I couldn't see how this situation would end up with anything other than him taking something from me that I didn't want to give. He carried me up the stairs, past a kitchen and a living room, and into a bathroom. He started to pull at my clothes, as if he wanted me to strip. I immediately burst into tears and tried to get away from him.

"You need to shower Eva," he said sharply.

"I'm not showering with you in here," I replied.

"It's either Anna, or it's me," he answered.

"Anna," I spit at him.

"I'll get her this time, but you need to get used to me touching you," he said before walking out of the bathroom.

I looked around the room, trying to see if there was anything I could hide in my clothes as some sort of weapon. Before I could search closely, the door creaked open wider and Anna walked into the room.

"Reverend Darcy asked me to watch you," she said stiffly, before settling herself on the toilet.

"I'm not changing in front of you, and are we allowed to close the door?" I asked, gesturing to the wide open door. She seemed to think for a second.

"I suppose that will be all right," she said, getting up to close the door.

She then returned to the toilet to continue staring at me. I got in the shower, closed the shower curtain and began to undress. I saw Anna's hand reach out as if to grab the curtain.

"Please, at least give me this," I said softly.

She paused, with her hand outstretched towards the curtain while she thought about my request. Finally, she retracted her hand and sat silently, giving me the go ahead to start my shower with some privacy. My clothes were stuck to my skin from the vomit, pee, and whatever other bodily fluids that had gotten on me while down in the basement for so long. It was a relief to strip them off although I didn't know what I was going to wear after the shower. I placed my clothes into a pile right outside the curtain, careful to keep it as closed as possible in case Anna got any ideas about needing to watch me again.

I turned on the shower and winced as the cold water sprayed all over me. I had gotten spoiled spending so much time at Damon and Beckham's places. His water temperature and pressure were always perfect. I laughed to myself, the quality of the shower was certainly not something I needed to be worrying about. A pang of loss welled up in me thinking about them.

Luckily there was shampoo and soap in the shower with me. I didn't have a washcloth, and didn't want to ask for one, so I rubbed the soap all over me, hoping that the soap hadn't touched a lot of other people. I noticed that there was a strange tingling sensation by my shoulder blades, I wondered if it had something to do with how I had been laying on the floor. I rubbed my back, trying to make the tingling go away.

I finally had delayed the shower for as long as it could go, and my skin was starting to prune. I turned the water there and stood there for a moment.

"Are there any towels I can use?" I tried to ask politely.

She stood up and opened up a cabinet under the sink, pulling out a towel. After she handed it to me, I wrapped it tightly around myself, not knowing what to do next, or if I was expected to put on my old clothes again. I reached out for the clothes. deciding it would be better to have those than have the Reverend see me in nothing but a towel.

"I have clothes for you," Anna said sharply.

I dropped the putrid clothes in my hand. She hesitated for a second before grabbing my bra that had been rolled up with the rest of my clothes. She then signaled for me to follow her out of the bathroom. I hesitated, fearful that he was going to be waiting out there for me.

"He's visiting with guests," she said, seeming to understand the look of indecision and fear on my face.

I followed her out of the bathroom, paying attention to my surroundings for the first time since I had come upstairs. We went the opposite way than we had come in, walking into a large room that appeared to be the master bedroom. Anna walked over to a door that opened into a closet. She looked through a few things before pulling out a pair of simple cotton underwear, a black long sleeve shirt, and what looked like leggings. She walked back towards me and handed me the clothes.

"Put these on," she told me.

I reluctantly grabbed the pile from her, uncomfortable with the thought of wearing her clothes. My bra smelled lightly of vomit, and I grimaced as I slipped it on, careful to keep the towel in front of me to shield my body from Anna's prying eyes.

After I was dressed, Anna led me back down the hallway. I could hear voices tersely discussing something as we approached a room at the end of the hallway. As we walked in, I immediately took a step backwards, beginning to tremble.

There in front of me, sitting stiffly on a leather backed sofa next to Reverend Darcy, were the Andersons. Mr. Anderson immediately stood up when he saw me, stepping towards me as if he couldn't contain himself.

"Sit down," ordered Reverend Darcy, his voice making it clear that it wasn't a request.

Anna gripped my arm and led me to a seat next to the Reverend. I examined Mr. and Mrs. Anderson. Both looked like they had aged dramatically somehow in the weeks that I had been gone. Mr. Anderson had a grey pallor that was drastically different from how I remembered him. What had happened to them?

"Eva. Your family has been very anxious for your return," he began. "When Patricia found you missing, she was beside herself. Your lack of respect for your mother and father is a sin. Proverbs 22:6. 'Honor your father and your mother, that your days may be long in the land that the Lord your God is giving you."

Despite the gravity of the situation I was in, I couldn't refrain from laughing a little and speaking out.

"They are not my father and mother. They are nothing more than abusive pigs," I snarled at him.

The Reverend looked taken aback at my outburst. "What do you mean "abusive"?" he replied in a cold voice that had the Andersons sitting up straight.

"What don't you understand about that word," I replied back, lifting my chin up firmly.

"I want you to describe what they did to you," he said, barely able to form words with his rage.

The Andersons had heard enough to cause them alarm apparently because Mrs. Anderson had stood up.

"We have never harmed a hair on that child's head," she gasped out.

"I would no sooner harm Eva than I would myself," said Mr. Anderson beseechingly.

The Reverend stood up, the look on his face so chilling that I wanted to run and hide despite the fact that it wasn't directed towards me.

Notwithstanding my hatred of them and all they had put me through for four years, I suddenly had the ludicrous urge to lie about what they had done, and pretend it was nothing. I hated the Andersons with all of my heart, but I couldn't find it in myself to wish for whatever torture I was sure the Reverend had in mind for them if I told him the truth.

"I wouldn't lie if I were you," the Reverend said, seeming to read my mind.

Maybe if I told him the truth he would feel sorry for me and let me go I thought. As far-fetched as it seemed, I was desperate for anything to change the Reverend's mind about keeping me his prisoner. I took a deep breath.

"For four years those people did whatever sadistic thing they could think of to me, whether it was cutting, or burning, or unwanted touches. I ran away because they had kept me locked in an attic almost since I arrived with them, and I wanted a better life than the abuse and neglect they were offering me."

The Reverend's face went strangely blank at my statement, as if my words had no effect on him whatsoever.

"That wasn't so hard was it," he said, in an eerily calm voice. Anna came back into the room just then. I hadn't noticed that she had left, she was so quiet.

"Dinner is ready," she announced.

The Reverend walked over to me, and held out his arm. I reluctantly stood up and placed my arm in his. We walked to a dining room which had been elegantly set. Despite everyone seeming familiar with this house, I didn't get the impression this was where Anna and the Reverend usually lived. Everything was dated and the house smelled musty, like it hadn't been used for quite some time.

From my brief impression of the Reverend at the Anderson's house, and the fact that he had been driving what looked like a very nice luxury car when he stopped by the house on the day I escaped, I was pretty sure they lived in a much nicer house than this. It gave me chills to think that he must have been planning something like this for sometime, or even worse, what if he had been using it for other girls before me.

I was led to a seat at the table. The Reverend pulled out my chair, and I gingerly sat down. I was still stiff and sore from my chair falling over in the basement.

"I'll be right back," he told the Andersons and me, signaling for them to take a seat. As soon as he was out of earshot, Mrs. Anderson launched into me.

"You ungrateful little bitch," she hissed. "When he comes back you are going to take back everything you said, or so help me I'll make sure something happens to you that you won't ever recover from."

I stared at her silently in response. Nothing I said would make a difference. The Andersons were just evil to their core. I made the mistake of looking at Mr. Anderson and did a double take. The difference in his appearance was startling. His skin color was back to a more normal shade. He looked younger and fresher. Glancing at Mrs. Anderson I saw that she seemed to be looking better as well. Was this some kind of power I had?

Reverend Darcy came in at that moment and I quickly looked over at him to see if he was recovering. Much to my astonishment he was looking much, much better than when he had first come down to my basement prison. What was doing this? A shiver went down my spine. Hopefully the fact that Beckham, Mason, and Damon were supernatural creatures would prevent it from happening to them. Mason had seemed fine so far on the tour away from me.

Thinking of the three men in my life sent a rush of agony through my heart. I wondered if I would ever see them again. I didn't expect that they would be riding in on white horses to save me anytime soon. I had never mentioned the Reverend to any of them. What I wouldn't give to be wrapped up in one of Damon's hugs, or get one of Mason's passionate kisses, or hear Beckham's sweet laugh.

My thoughts were interrupted by Anna bringing soup bowls into the room. She set bowls down in front of the Andersons first, and then served the Reverend and I before serving herself. She then sat down to the right of the Reverend. The Reverend still had the same eerily calm look on his face. The Andersons had dug into their soup with gusto. Watching them eat reminded me that I was starving since I had puked everything in my stomach up earlier.

I picked up my soup spoon, deciding that I needed to keep my strength up in case an opportunity to escape presented itself. As I opened my mouth to eat, I realized how strange it was that the Reverend hadn't demanded that we say a prayer prior to eating. I was sure that we had prayed when he had visited the Anderson's house before. Out of the corner of my eye I saw that Anna was sitting with her hands folded in her lap, looking down sorrowfully. Meanwhile, the Reverend had begun eating, not seeming to notice his wife's distress.

I again was about to take a sip of my soup when I heard a choking sound from across the table. I dropped my spoon, making a loud clang as it hit the bowl, and looked over at the Andersons. Mr. Anderson was making a choking/gagging sound. Foam was dribbling from his mouth, and his eyes had gone bloodshot. He was grasping his neck as if something was stuck in his throat.

Mrs. Anderson started screaming, and began to pat him

on his back. She was forced to stop her efforts when she too grabbed her throat and started to make choking sounds. A dribble of foam started to come out of her mouth as well. I stood up quickly, and looked over at the Reverend. He was serenely eating his soup as if nothing was happening at the table.

"What did you do?" I cried out to him. "Please help them!"

"Sit down Eva," the Reverend said in a voice that gave no room for argument.

Ignoring him, I raced around the table. He stood up.

"I said sit down," he yelled in a voice that felt like thunder. I glared at him, and started hitting both of the Andersons on the back, hoping that it would help them to throw up something, and get the poison (or whatever it was), out of them. The Reverend abruptly stood up, walked over to me, and dragged me back to my seat while Mr. and Mrs. Anderson continued to suffer what seemed like agonizing pain. I was plopped forcefully into my seat. The Reverend pulled handcuffs out of his pocket, and handcuffed one of my hands to the side of my chair, ensuring that I wouldn't be able to go anywhere.

The next thirty minutes were the most gruesome and frightening moments of my life. As I sat chained to my chair, Mr. and Mrs. Anderson continued to suffer and slowly die in front of me. Their faces turned a withered grey, green mix. Towards the end both of them started to bleed from their eyes and ears. I knew this moment would haunt my dreams for years to come.

When death finally came for Mr. and Mrs. Anderson, I felt immense relief that their suffering had ended. My mind was having a difficult time comprehending the fact that I had just been forced to watch someone die in front of me. And not just die, but basically be tortured to death in one of the most ghastly ways imaginable. I felt like I had stepped into an alternate reality, one filled with nightmares. How was it possible that I had just been laughing with Damon, and blushing over some text that Mason had sent over?

I began to shiver, I felt like I was freezing to death. I wanted to cry, but I felt frozen from the shock of what I had just witnessed. My back continued to feel strange, as if the muscles were twitching underneath my skin. My bones felt like they wanted to rip through. I shifted uncomfortably in my chair. I was starting to lose feeling in the hand that was handcuffed to my chair.

I looked over at the Reverend. He had just finished taking his last bite of soup, and Anna was collecting his bowl with shaking hands. He looked over at me with an amused look.

"Aren't you going to finish your soup?" he asked in a seemingly solicitous voice, like two corpses weren't sitting across the table from us.

I gaped at him. The Reverend had given me a bad feeling when I had first met him, but nothing could have prepared me for the evil I could now see radiating from his soul.

"Don't look so alarmed my dear as if I'm some kind of monster. What just happened is a biblical principal that was commanded by God," he explained, the same amused look on his face as if my reaction was out of the ordinary.

I stared at him aghast. I hadn't really ever been to church. None of my foster families had been interested except for the Andersons, and they certainly weren't going to take me out in public like that would have required. However, I had skimmed over some of the verses here and there, and I couldn't remember it ever saying that you were supposed to murder people.

"Leviticus 24 is just one of the many chapters that I'm talking about my dear. 'Breach for breach, eye for eye, tooth for tooth: as he hath caused a blemish in a man, so shall it be done to him again.' It's all laid out very clear," he explained as if what he was saying made perfect sense.

I opened my mouth and then closed it again, not knowing what exactly to say to explain how crazy what he had just said was. As evil as the Andersons were, they had obviously never poisoned me to death. I felt the thick taste of guilt in my mouth. If I hadn't said anything, than this wouldn't have happened. I was basically a murderer.

Before I could get anything out, Anna arrived with more plates. She set salads in front of both the Reverend and I, her hands still shaking so hard that the silverware clattered against the sides of the plates. The Reverend sent her an admonishing look. Anna took a deep breath in what looked like an effort to calm down, but failed miserably. I didn't blame her. My insides felt like a sack of snakes had been let loose inside them.

The next hour stretched on for what seemed like forever. Mr. and Mrs. Anderson's corpses sat in front of me. Mrs. Anderson had died looking at me, with one of her hands outstretched on the table. I couldn't keep my eyes off of it. It seemed to be stretching towards me, a visual reminder that I had caused her death. The Reverend had Anna bring out three more courses before he finished with dinner. He ate painstakingly slow, as if it was his goal for me to spend as much time possible in this room, the lesson of what happened when he was crossed engrained in my mind for all eternity.

He finally stood up. Like me, Anna hadn't touched any of the food on the table. The Reverend clicked his tongue in disappointment at our full plates.

"It is a sin to be wasteful," he counseled us.

Anna nodded her head in agreement, but made no move to eat. I just stared at him, still not comprehending the lunacy that continued to come out of his mouth.

"I'm sure you are exhausted my dear," he said to me. "Anna

will show you to your room. We have had it specially prepared for you."

He walked over to me and unlocked my handcuff, taking my wrist in his hand and massaging it. I felt dirty where he touched me, and it took everything inside of me not to visibly cringe. After he apparently felt satisfied that the blood had returned to my hand, he leaned over and placed a kiss on my cheek. This time I couldn't help but flinch and I immediately felt his anger at my reaction. He must have felt that I had been traumatized enough by the evening though, so he didn't say anything. His eyes held the promise that I would regret it if my actions continued.

I wondered what he was going to do with the bodies. I shuddered thinking that I would have to sleep under the same roof as the corpses. I wouldn't blame them if they came back alive and choked me in my sleep. I was sure that there would be plenty of haunting going on. Anna was waiting by the door for me to follow her. I felt the Reverend's eyes follow me out of the room, and I couldn't help but give a sigh of relief as I left at the fact that I was no longer in that hell-scape.

Twenty-Six

Anna led me back down the hallway, past the bathroom, and into a small bedroom. I stared in confusion at the room around me. It almost looked like a kitchy honeymoon suite, like the kind at low-budget motels. I only knew this because one of the better foster families, pre-Andersons, had attempted to take me on a family road-trip with their kids. It had ended up being a disaster. The car had broken down and needed to go in a repair shop while we were in the middle of nowhere. The motel we were forced to stay in while the car was fixed had surprisingly only had one room available, their version of a honeymoon suite. I remember it had been decked out in red velvet with a lot of white and black trim. This room was similar.

The furniture was all black, but the bedding, curtains, lamp shades...basically everything else, was a blood red, and seemed to be made of some sort of velvet material. It all seemed strangely out of place in the house. Everything looked more expensive than anything else I had seen in the other rooms. A shiver went down my spine. I felt like I wasn't understanding something.

Anna cleared her throat behind me and I jumped. I had forgotten she was in the room with me.

"Do you need to use the restroom before bed?" she asked quietly.

I sighed. I had ended up in the same kind of prison as before, albeit a prison with more decorations. I nodded, not able to speak after the horror I had just witnessed. There was another bathroom attached to the bedroom. Anna followed me into it, "kindly" averting her eyes while I did my business. I supposed that they were worried I would find something to help me escape if they left me alone for even a minute. Looking around the bathroom I didn't see anything that looked like it would be useful in escaping at all.

After I finished, Anna led me back into the bedroom where she bid me goodnight, and locked the door behind herself. After I heard her footsteps fade down the hall, I went to the doorknob to see if it was similar to the one at the Anderson's, and could be picked. Much to my dismay it looked like a heavyweight deadbolt lock had been installed recently. I wondered if Reverend Darcy had picked the Anderson's brain about my escape.

Thinking of the Andersons made me want to puke. I gingerly got into the bed, sniffing the sheets first to see if they smelled okay. I really didn't have a right to be picky. This bed was worlds better than the basement floor I had slept the night before, or the cot that I had slept in for four years with the Andersons.

I pulled the covers up, but couldn't keep my eyes closed. Visions of the ghastly dinner party twirled through my brain. I kept seeing how the Andersons twitched, the retching noises they made, and the blood that dripped from their eyes. I began to sob, overcome with the horror of the night. My back muscles began to twitch again, and I shifted uncomfortably. I wondered if they were just protesting from my uncomfortable position in the basement. I would have thought I would have healed from that already.

I tried to think of anything else to get my mind off of the nightmare I was in, but I could feel a panic attack rising within me. My breath started to speed up, and I started hiccupping while I cried.

A whisper of frost caressed my cheek. Another specter was near. I took a deep breath, the cold air filled my lungs. An icy touch, and then...

The guard had spent his entire long life watching the queen. He had loved her since he was a child and thought of himself as her most loyal guard. He would have done anything for her, given her anything. Watching her light fade away was tortuous.

"Ailean," the Queen's weak voice called out. The guard rushed to her side.

"Yes, your majesty?" he asked.

He shivered as she laid a hand on his cheek, and brought him near to her. She was burning up with fever.

"I'm afraid that my daughter is in grave danger," she told him, her eyes staring deeply into his. "I need you to go get her and bring her to my chambers. I need to keep her safe while I am able."

The guard knew this wasn't possible. The Princess wasn't here. She had left on urgent palace business earlier this morning. He had no idea where she had went, and was hesitant to leave the Queen's side to find out, not when she was so weak.

"The Princess left this morning, my Queen," the guard told her hesitantly.

Panic slid over the Queen's features. "When will she be back? I have to do it, I have to protect her," she said feverishly, madness filling her eyes.

She kept repeating the same statements while the guard tried uselessly to calm her. He finally had to have another guard call for Brianag, the Queen's personal witch, to have her bring something to help the Queen sleep.

The Queen's admonitions to the guard disappeared from his mind in his anxiety over her health. He could tell by Brianag's face that there wasn't much time left.

After the vision I stayed awake for most of the night going over what I had seen for the millionth time. The specters were obviously memories from the same place I had kept dreaming about. But what did all of it mean? And why did I keep seeing it?

I must have finally drifted off to sleep during the night, because I woke up to hear the lock clicking on the door. Anna stepped through the doorway.

"The Reverend has requested your presence," she told me, as stiffly as the night before.

I nodded and got out of the bed. Anna laid out a rather revealing black dress for me to change into. I could tell she disapproved whole heartedly of how much skin the dress showed, and I agreed with her. I just knew that I was going to feel dirty all day long if I had to sit in front of the Reverend in this dress. Despite my disgust, I slipped it on. The thought of the Anderson's faces twisting in agony preventing me from pushing back too hard against the Reverend's desires.

Anna led me to the dining room table. An assortment of breakfast dishes lay on the table. I waited for the Reverend to appear, but when Anna silently prayed and then began picking at her food, I realized he wasn't coming. I went to take a bite of some eggs, but stopped suddenly, images of the Andersons both foaming and convulsing at the table making me lose my appetite even though I hadn't eaten in days.

If Anna noticed that I wasn't eating, she didn't say anything. We both sat there in awkward silence until she looked at the clock and finally stood up.

"Follow me please," she said.

She put a hand on my arm, as if to ensure that I wouldn't run away. She led me into an office. Much to my dismay, the Reverend was sitting at a large mahogany desk, scribbling away at something.

"Take that chair, and set it in front of the desk please," he told Anna, motioning to a padded seat off to the side of the room. Once she had done as he asked, he motioned for me to sit in it. Thus, started one of the more bizarre days of my life.

The Reverend sat for most of the day behind his desk, preparing what I soon realized was a sermon. He would frequently stare at me, going over something in his mind before he resumed writing, and muttering random bible verses to himself. He didn't talk to me, only speaking to Anna when he wanted her to bring us something. My body ached from sitting on the hard wooden chair for so long, and my back twitched continually with the weird sensation.

My anger at Anna rapidly faded throughout the day. I realized she was just as much of a prisoner as I was. When she wasn't doing the Reverend's bidding, she sat in a chair in a corner, reading from what looked like a bible. After several hours of writing, the Reverend finally stood up.

"Anna, accompany Eva to her room, and then return to me please. I have several important matters to attend to."

The Reverend seemed preoccupied as he said this, staring at me intensely like I held the key to something he was trying to figure out. Anna led me to my room, and locked me inside once again after allowing me to use the restroom.

Unlike the day before, Anna brought a tray to me for dinner. I was grateful to eat away from the dining room, and scarfed down the sandwich and salad she had brought me, so hungry that I only gave a fleeting thought to the fact that the Reverend could have easily put poison in it.

I didn't hear from anyone until the next morning. The silence was maddening as my mind concocted various horrors that the Reverend was preparing for me. My fragile nerves were put more on edge by Anna's demeanor when she came to get me the next morning.

Anna was twitchy. Her eyes glancing nervously at me and then away, as if she had something to say but was too afraid to get the words out. After a silent breakfast in the dining room, I was led back into the study to sit again directly in front of the Reverend while he worked on his sermon.

Unlike the day before however, the Reverend only wrote for a few hours before standing up abruptly.

"I have errands to attend to," he announced to us, his eyes shining gleefully for some reason.

I thought he would have Anna lead me back to my bedroom, but immediately tensed when he pulled the same pair of thick silver cuffs from before, out of one of his desk drawers. He walked over to me, and fastened my left wrist to the side of the chair. The metal chafed at my skin, and I gave him a furious look.

"Don't fret my sweet," he said to me. "I'm allowing you to stay out today as a sign of my trust. Anna will be reading several sermons to you today to begin your church education."

He gave me a perfunctory kiss on my cheek which made me gag once again, before striding out of the room without another word or a parting glance at his wife.

Twenty-Seven

Anna walked to the window, watching as the Reverend drove away. She stayed there for about ten minutes until she turned to me swiftly.

"You need to go," she said urgently.

I stared at her dumbly, unsure of why she was saying this now.

"He kept the key to your lock, I'm going to have to find a way to pick it."

She ran out of the room briefly, before returning a minute later holding a pin. She began to jab it in. She obviously had no experience picking locks with the savage way she was attacking it. I finally woke up from the stupor her sudden change of heart had put me in, and motioned for her to hand me the pin. I set about trying to trip the lock like I had in doors before. Unfortunately, this handcuff seemed to be specially made, and I couldn't figure out how to do it. Anna was pacing by the window, wringing her hands. She looked over to me.

"Is it working?" she asked anxiously.

"No!" I said, panic starting to thread through my voice as I saw my window of opportunity to escape rapidly disappearing. Anna was now chewing on her fingernails.

"Do you have any other tools you can think of?" I asked her.

I looked down at the chair I was in. The Reverend had brought a wooden kitchen chair into the living room because it was easier to lock me to it than the padded furniture that comprised the rest of the room. The spindles of the chair didn't look that sturdy. I wondered if I could maybe break them. I began to yank as hard as I could on the rod, only succeeding in spraining my wrist in the process.

"What about a saw of some sort?" I gasped out, my voice going raspy with excitement at the idea.

Anna nodded and ran out of the room. I heard a door open somewhere in the house. I wondered if she had gone in a garage or something. She came back holding a large saw that was rusted with age, perspiration lining her brow. I looked at it shakily. There was no way that I could hold that with one hand. I was going to have to trust Anna that she wouldn't cut one of my body parts off while she attempted to cut the chair.

Anna hustled over to my chair and sank down on her knees. She began to move the saw slowly, careful to stay out of range of my hand which was dangling by the chair where it was connected by the cuff. It became obvious to both of us that cutting the chair was going to require a lot more force than she was using now. She looked at me worried, and I nodded my head, gritting my teeth for the off chance that the saw slid and she cut me instead.

She began to saw faster, sweat dripping profusely from her brow now. Anna was a small woman, much shorter than me, with a slight build. I'm sure that moving the giant saw was very difficult for her, and I admired her effort. Every so often Anna would stop, and we would both listen worriedly for the sound of a car announcing the Reverend's return.

After Anna had been sawing for a few minutes, I began to start pulling on the cuff to help try and break the wood. It still held on strong though, and I had to stop for fear the cuff was going to break my skin and I would start bleeding. Beckham had said that I didn't have hemophilia, but that my blood probably held power instead. I wasn't ready to test that theory in this situation.

Anna continued to saw, making very little progress as the saw seemed to be very rusted and dull. I began to panic. I felt like the Reverend was going to be back any time now. I pulled again on my cuff anxiously, and this time was pleased when I heard a cracking sound, like the wood was splintering under the pressure. This seemed to spur Anna forward, and she started sawing feverishly. I jumped multiple times as the saw came very close to nicking my wrist.

Finally, after one more pull from me, the wooden chair leg broke. I was free!

"Hurry," Anna cried, pulling me off of the chair and pulling me out into the hallway.

She led me through the kitchen where there was a back door. She stopped us at the door, and grabbed a bag that had been half-hazardly stuck in the space between the fridge and the cabinet.

"I packed some food in here for you," she said as she gave me the bag. "It's not much, but it will hopefully last you until you find a phone and can call someone. I don't have a phone to give you. The Reverend doesn't let me have a cell phone, and I haven't been able to find any phones anywhere in the house."

"Why are you doing this?" I asked, slightly suspicious of her motives.

"He has something terrible planned for you," she answered. "Something that is surely a sin against God."

"What is it?" I asked, dread clawing at my throat.

"There's not time, you need to go!"

"Where are we?" I said hurriedly. "Which way should I go?"

I had no idea how long I had been out between when I was knocked out, and when I woke up in the basement. What if we were back in Illinois or something?

"We're in upstate New York, outside of a little town called Norwich. I'm not familiar with the area at all. He hadn't had me arrive until a day before he brought you here," Anna said. She began to tear up. "Eva, I am so sorry how I treated you when you first arrived. I was so jealous of you. You don't know what it's been like, seeing your husband so obsessed with another woman. Obsessed doesn't even seem strong enough a word for how he has been about you."

She began to sob, great gasping cries that tore at my heart.

"Come with me. You can get away from him too," I said pleadingly. She straightened her shoulders. "I promised 'till death do we part.' I will not abandon my vows," she said, her lips trembling.

I couldn't help but give her a quick hug. I had so much gratefulness to her. Finally, the urgency of the situation came back to me, and I pulled away from her. I opened the door and took one last look back at her before heading out the door, hopefully never to see this nightmare again.

I started jogging as soon as I stepped off the back porch, aware that I had lost precious time with that last interlude with Anna. My heart ached at the thought of her facing the Reverend's wrath alone. When I reunited with the guys I would bring them back with me, and have them help me drag her away if that's what it took.

The house was surrounded by a dense forest. It was slow going trying to pick my way carefully through the trees and dense underbrush. Gnats swirled around me, I was sure I had eaten at least a dozen.

I walked for what seemed like hours. The forest grew dimmer as the day passed. The Reverend had left a few hours after lunch but it had taken quite a bit of time to get me loose from that chair, and with how long I had been walking I was sure it would get dark soon. I shivered at the thought of sleeping in the forest alone. The forest had been mostly silent as I walked, with the exception of a few birds chirping from up above. Every so often I thought I heard a beeping sound. I couldn't find where it was coming from though and thought I must be imagining it.

As the light faded, the forest began to come alive. Strange growls and the crunching of leaves nearby had me trying to walk faster...which led to several trips and falls. I was filthy from how muddy the forest floor was. The tennis shoes that Anna had given me were soaked in mud. Moisture had seeped into the shoes, and I had gotten several blisters. My wrist was chafed from where the handcuff kept rubbing against it.

Any light had almost completely disappeared when I finally saw a break in the trees up ahead. I heard some cars driving by, and almost cried in relief. I reached the edge of the tree line and peered out. The road was surrounded on both sides by forest. I could probably get away with walking on the edge of the forest so that I wasn't seen and still be able to follow the road. Eventually it had to lead through a town right?

The road stretched on forever. I was exhausted, but I had the terrible feeling that if I dared to stop the Reverend would find me. Occasionally a car would drive by and I would lunge deeper into the trees so I wouldn't be spotted. I had been walking for what seemed like several hours when I came to a section of the road that turned into a bridge due to a large ravine. I was going to have to leave my safe spot at the edge of the forest and walk on the bridge in order to keep going. Thoughts of finally getting to a phone and being able to call for help propelled me forward. I waited in the trees, listening to see if any cars were nearby. When all I heard was silence, I hesitantly began to walk as quickly as I could across the bridge. My head began to spin from looking over the side of the bridge, the ravine had quite the drop.

As was my luck, I heard a car approaching from behind me. I started jogging, hoping to be able to get to the other side of the ravine before it got close. I was just about across the bridge when the car arrived. It sped past me, not slowing down at all. I breathed out a sigh of relief. I was being too paranoid. The Reverend wasn't going to find me. I heard another faint beep. It sounded like it was coming from inside of me. I patted my clothes but didn't feel anything. The light was very dim now, but I held up the handcuff to see if I could see anything on it. It looked like regular metal to me. I rolled my shoulders back and continued on.

It was pitch black now. The Reverend had done a good job of buying a house in the middle of nowhere. I had never been anywhere as remote as this. There weren't any lights along the road. I was lucky that there was an almost full moon or I would have probably gotten myself killed walking into another ravine. My back was still feeling strange, and I kept looking over my shoulder, peering into the darkness for the eyes I kept imagining were watching me. Nothing was ever there.

I finally decided I was going to have to find some shelter a little deeper in the forest, away from the road, so that I could sleep for a few hours. I walked a few feet into the forest and found a wide tree. I shuddered at the thought of the creepy crawlies that I was sure where all over it. I was actually grateful for the dark from hiding them from view.

Anna had given me a small windbreaker before I left. I contemplated whether I should take it off and use it for a pillow, or keep it on to try and protect myself from the cold.

Now that it was September, the nights were getting freezing. It didn't help that my clothes were soaked with water and mud. I decided that I would use a pile of leaves as a pillow and keep the coat on for some warmth.

After choking down an apple, I laid down in a pile of dead leaves. I was exhausted. It was the kind of exhaustion that you could feel in your bones. Tears leaked out of my eyes despite my best efforts to stop myself from crying. I had never felt so alone. I had no idea how far away I was from civilization, let alone if I was actually heading the right way to actually reach civilization. The dark played tricks with my mind. I envisioned various ghastly beasts and monsters surrounding me. Every rustle of leaves and cracking of branches made me jump. Besides being cold and uncomfortable from laying on the ground, my back continued to twitch and ache as well. It felt like something was waiting to burst out of my skin.

My mind kept whirling, and I could feel another panic attack coming on. Suddenly the air grew even frostier and silence took over my senses. I knew the score...a specter was nearby. I didn't have the energy to yell at it. I waited patiently for it to come nearer, resigned in knowing that another sorrowful vision would be coming soon.

As the forest was so dark, I could only see the bare outline of the specter as it leaned closer to me. I braced myself for the icy touch. This one laid its whole hand on my face and a tremor went down my spine.

I lived for stolen moments like these. Lexi had arranged for me to disappear for the weekend, citing urgent business I had to attend to in the north. I had left the castle with pomp and glory, riding out with several armed guards to make sure it looked like I was heading towards official palace business. A few miles out, once we reached a quiet, sheltered portion of the forest that was safe from inquiring eyes, my guards veered left, nodding as they passed me. I was once again grateful for their loyalty as I headed the opposite direction.

I had been given directions of where I was going, and I rode hard, the anticipation of seeing Beckham after weeks of being forced to stay away lighting a fire beneath me. It was two hours before I finally reached the spot where we were to meet. My directions had led me to a clearing. A thatched cottage stood tall before me. I was immediately entranced by its beauty. The walls of the cottage were a smooth cream material, and lush, thick, flowering vines wrapped their way up the walls. The roof was made up of what looked like burnt red tiles, and a charming chimney rose from it. It was also covered in the gorgeous vines, and a thin trail of smoke danced out from its depths. I was delighted that Beckham had chosen such a charming spot for our rendezvous.

I was inexplicably nervous as I approached the door. I took a deep breath, but before I could knock, the door swung open and Beckham was there, sweeping me into his arms. He gave me a kiss that was so ardent I knew that he had felt the pain of the last few weeks without each other just as much as I had. When our kisses began to head us in a more serious direction, Beckham finally pulled away from me.

"Hi," he said, flashing that smile that always made my heart start beating faster.

"Hi," I answered, taking a moment to observe his beauty. Growing up my mother had told me stories of beings worshipped in other worlds. My favorite stories were always about the gods of Mt. Olympus. When she was young, before she had married Father, Mother had once had an affair with the leader of the Mt. Olympus gods, Zeus. She often regaled me with the stories about everything that happened during that time, but I especially loved hearing stories about Apollo, the god of the sun. Beckham looked how I had always imagined Apollo when Mother told me those tales. Gold skin, gold hair, gleaming blue

eyes that were brighter than the Capian Sea beyond my palace. Every time I looked at him I was grateful he was mine. The fact that he was as golden on the inside as he was on the outside pushed him as close to perfection as I could imagine.

Bringing me back from my musings, Beckham took my hand and led me into the cottage. I immediately fell even further in love with the place. While I couldn't complain about the palace, its gleaming white marble walls were sometimes cold, especially with the current company. This place on the other hand felt warm and snug.

As Beckham took me on a tour of the cottage, I decided that this would definitely be considered the perfect spot for a love nest. There were squishy couches and arm chairs set around a large stone fireplace, with plenty of throw pillows to lounge on. The floors were made of gleaming, brown wood. The walls were white, but the kind of white that looked aged and lived in. A table for two was set next to a quaint kitchen with white cupboards and a red accented island. There was an office, or small recreational room that held a wall of books down the hallway.

I stopped short when he led me to the main bedroom. The bedroom was in the back corner of the cottage, and light streamed in from large windows on two of the walls, bathing the room in the glow from the sunset. There were wispy, gauzy, white curtains around the bed. They were waving slightly from the breeze coming in from an open window. I was enchanted. Suddenly standing in front of the bed with Beckham avidly watching me was too much, so I walked swiftly out of the room with him following closely behind.

"Everything alright?" he asked, a knowing smile on his face.

"In this moment, everything is perfect," I answered honestly.

Lexi had arranged for me to have two days with Beckham. We spent the first day cuddling every second we could, talking about anything and everything. He took me to a stream nearby where we leisurely fished for dinner, our toes dangling in the icy water. Curled up in front of the fire that first night, Beckham read to me. I fell asleep with my head on his lap, his fingers tenderly stroking my hair as he read happy tales to me where love always prevailed.

We spent the second day much the same as the first, leisurely and lovingly. Beckham took me on a horseback ride to a meadow where wildflowers of every kind grew. Beckham watched me in amazement as I grew even more flowers instantaneously, my power slowly growing as my mother's waned. A part of me had been hesitant to leave her side, but now I realized that a small break from my sobering reality was exactly what I had needed.

As our last night together drew closer, there was urgency in our actions. Every touch, every word, grew more important. We both knew it was unclear when we would be able to steal a moment away with Lord Tiberius and Father watching my every movement.

We had stayed, wrapped in each other's arms for most of the evening after cooking a simple supper together. We finally ventured into the bedroom where I fell quickly into a fitful rest, the reality of the next day looming large in my dreams.

I woke right as dawn was breaking. Beckham was lying facing me, and I took advantage of the opportunity to admire him. His long eyelashes lay curled against the gold of his cheek. His blonde hair was tousled in his sleep and adorably went every which way. My eyes were drawn down to his naked chest. His sculpted chest making its way down to the yummiest six pack the world had ever seen. I was startled when he suddenly spoke.

"Admiring the view angel?" he said in a raspy, just woken up voice.

"Always," I whispered. His eyes opened, sensing the deeper meaning beneath my reply. With the curtains once again dancing around us in the breeze from the window we had left

open, and the soft morning light resting softly upon us, I felt like I was in a dream. This was the moment.

Beckham must have seen the thoughts in my gaze as he soon reached for me. He laid soft kisses on my lips that quickly turned more and more passionate as if we couldn't get enough of one another. Standing up and looking into his eyes, I slowly slid the bands of my satin nightgown off my shoulder, the gown slipping off the rest of my body and pooling at my feet. Beckham drank me in, his face portraying a look of awe and worshipful love.

"Are you sure?" he asked me, his voice so full of aching and longing that I could almost taste it.

"I've never been surer of anything," I responded.

Although we had been in love for years, we had never taken this step. Beckham had always been content to wait, wanting me to mature and be sure before I made the decision that he was the one. I was after all destined to be his queen, and could have my pick of anyone. But since meeting Beckham, no one else had even become a thought. He was my everything.

I slowly crawled towards where he had sat up in bed, his hands clenching with the need to haul me towards him. I kneeled before him, brushing my lips against his and roving my hands in discovery all over his perfect physique. Beckham finally reached the end of his control, pulling me towards him and beginning an exploration of my body that left me breathless and crying out. He flipped me beneath him, his body hovering over me, held slightly up so as not to crush me beneath him. His eyes peered into my soul as we finally became one. Soft sighs turned into cries of passion.

"I'll love no one else for eternity," he breathlessly promised me as he moved over me. Before I could answer, a rush of pleasure moved through me, making me cry out in bliss. Beckham soon followed me into its depths.

We laid there afterwards, staring into each other's eyes, murmuring whispered endearments. I didn't know how anything else could possibly top this moment. In this moment there was room for nothing else but complete joy and happiness.

The happiness didn't even fade as we were forced to say goodbye. Beckham decided to leave at the same time, unable to stay in the cottage without me, afraid that my absence would spoil the place for him. I rode off first, with him promising to follow at a discreet distance behind. I took one last look at the cottage, I felt like I had been forever changed from my time between its walls. Taking a deep breath, I turned my horse around and rode hard back to real life.

Twenty-Eight

I woke suddenly. The beeping that had been bothering me periodically had all of a sudden gotten louder and more insistent. I sat up with a slight groan. Despite the warmth of the vision, or whatever it was that I had seen, the cold of the ground had still crawled further into my bones. I wasn't sure that I would ever be warm again. Light had started to filter in through the treetops. I was amazed that I had managed to sleep so long. I sent a silent thank you to the specter who had brought me such a happy moment.

As was becoming my routine, I started patting myself down, trying to find where the beeping was coming from. It couldn't be good that it was growing louder. I was worried that the beeping was connected to some kind of tracker, and I cursed myself for sleeping so late and allowing the Reverend time to most likely get closer.

At that thought, I heard voices coming from nearby. I stood quickly, grabbing the backpack Anna had given me. I began to jog, as quietly as possible, hoping that I could get some distance away. Sticks and branches scratched me as I rushed by.

This went on for an hour until finally I couldn't hear the voices anymore. I decided to venture closer to the road again so that I could make sure I was heading in the right direction. The light grew brighter as I neared the tree line. I could occasionally hear cars driving past, but like the night before, there didn't seem to be very many.

I decided to again stay within the tree line, trying to jog as fast as possible. I was grateful for my ability to run without stopping for long periods. I couldn't have imagined I would need it for a situation like this though. Another hour passed. I had once again run into a bridge with a deep ravine underneath it. I moved out of tree line to examine it closer. It couldn't be...it was the same bridge I had encountered the night before. I had somehow gone in a circle while running from the voices in the woods.

My insides started quivering. I took a deep breath, trying to hold back the tears that were once again threatening to erupt out of me. I heard a car approaching. I didn't even move as it stopped in front of me. I knew who it was. The beeping was now a loud shrill that was going off incessantly. The Reverend stepped out of the car and walked towards me. I felt frozen in despair and disgust.

He grabbed my arm and frog marched me back to the car. I finally snapped out of the daze of finding out that I hadn't actually gained any ground, and started trying to yank away from his grasp. Staying seemingly calm, he pulled a silver gun out of a holster that I hadn't noticed was around his waist. He put it against my forehead and held my eyes with his.

"Let me make something clear Eva. The thought of ending your life is so awful to me that I would have to follow you into death's depths if it were to happen. However, the thought of you being away from me, or with anyone else, is something that I can absolutely not tolerate. So make your choice, either choose to come with me now, or choose to end your life...and mine...right now."

A small part of me just wanted it to be over. Whatever the Reverend had planned for me, I'm sure it was going to make me wish for death a million times over. Suddenly, the vision from the night before floated into my brain. Somewhere out there, Beckham, Mason, and Damon still lived. While I lived, there was always a chance that a miracle could happen, and I could be reunited with them. If I chose to die right now, that chance would be gone.

I must have taken too long to decide. The Reverend cocked his gun, and his finger moved to the trigger.

"Wait!" I cried.

He grew still.

"I'll go with you," I told him in a resigned voice.

"Are you sure?" he asked. "I will not be lenient next time if anything like this happens again."

"I'm sure," I answered. He led me to the car, locking my handcuff to a hook on my seat before closing the door.

The car ride was silent on the way back. I wondered how far I had made it and how long it would take to get back to the house. My thoughts turned to Anna. How was she faring? Surely he hadn't killed his wife for helping me...right? She could have made up an excuse that I had broken the chair leg. Maybe he would have believed that?

My thoughts were cut off when the house came into view. It had only taken about an hour to get back. So much effort wasted. We pulled into the driveway and the Reverend finally spoke.

"I had been wanting to wait for you to come to this conclusion naturally. But your actions have left me no choice but to move forward," he said.

"What are talking about?" I asked, thoroughly confused.

Despite my confusion, dread rose in my throat in anticipation of whatever he was going to say next.

"When we go inside you are going back to the basement. There will be no more special treatment."

I shuddered thinking of the cold, stark basement that I had woken up in only a few nights ago.

"You will wait there until I have everything prepared," he continued.

"Prepared for what?" I asked hesitantly. He grunted in answer and got out of the car. After retrieving me he led me down the narrow basement steps. Everything was as it had been left, even the pool of vomit that I had lain in before I had been retrieved. He led me to the mattress, and moved my cuff to connect around my ankle before connecting it to a chain that was connected to the ground. It looked like it would give me about enough room to walk to the bucket in the corner to use the restroom.

I settled on the mattress and stared at the floor, feeling unsettled that the Reverend was so close to me while I was on a bed. He crouched down in front of me and tilted up my chin so I was looking at him.

"Just in case your pretty little head gets any more ideas. You have a tracker inserted right here," he said, brushing his finger against my left shoulder. I took a deep breath. That must have been why my shoulder hurt when I had first woken up after being captured. My healing abilities must have erased the mark before I could see it. No wonder the beeping was so easy to hear. It was right by my ear.

The Reverend stood up and began to walk away. Unable to help myself I cried out, "Reverend, please don't leave me down here!" He turned to look at me.

"Eva, I've said this before...call me Kylan," he answered, before turning and briskly walking back up the stairs. He flipped a switch and the basement was plunged into darkness. My punishment had begun.

Twenty-Nine

I had been sitting on the dirty mattress, my ankle chained to the floor, for a few hours. I hadn't heard anything from upstairs, and I wondered what was going on. My stomach growled, I longingly thought of the apple that was in Anna's backpack. My shoulders twitched for the millionth time since I had been taken, and I reached behind my back to massage them, trying to provide myself some relief. No matter what I did, the feeling didn't go away.

The basement light clicked on and I jumped, the chain clattering with my movement. Footsteps sounded down the stairs. The Reverend came into view. He kneeled in front of me.

"Have you had an attitude change yet, my darling?" he asked me. I stared at him, not saying anything. He seemed nonplussed by my silence.

"Everything has been arranged. Tonight, we will finally be joined as one," he announced. I gaped at him.

"Joined as one?" I asked, stupidly not understanding his intent.

"You are to become my wife. Proverbs 18:22 Eva, 'He who

finds a wife finds a good thing and obtains favor from the Lord,'" the Reverend stated with delight.

"I'm pretty sure that verse doesn't apply to your plans seeing as how you already have a wife," I answered saucily, wondering where Anna was.

Fear rose up in my chest. He had no issue with disposing of the Andersons because of actions he hadn't even seen them do. What would happen to Anna, who had actively gone against his orders? Was she still alive? Tears slid down my cheeks unhindered thinking of the courage that Anna had displayed in blatantly risking her life to help me. I noticed a spot of blood on the Reverend's pants. I hoped foolishly that the spot was from something other than Anna.

"I'm going to give you a little more time to get used to this idea while I prepare our room," he said patiently, ignoring everything I'd just said. "I'll be back in a few hours to collect you for our new life."

With that, he stood up, brushed his knees off, and walked back up the stairs. The basement was once again plunged into darkness.

What was I going to do? Would I be considered married under the law even if I didn't say yes, if it was all coerced? I started frantically pulling at the chain. I wanted to call out for help but I knew it would be a wasted effort. I didn't want Anna to help me even if she was able to hear me for fear that something would happen to her...if something hadn't happened already.

No matter how hard I pulled, the chain didn't budge. Obviously if I was some kind of supernatural, I wasn't one that had supernatural strength.

I finally gave up on trying to break the chain. I drew my knees up to my chest and laid my head down on them despondently. I wondered what day it was. Was it my birthday yet?

I wondered if Damon, Mason, and Beckham were

searching for me. It would probably be better for them if I disappeared forever. That way they wouldn't have to deal with me being in love with all of them, and they could each choose to have someone who loved just them.

I shook my head, angry at myself for such depressing thoughts. All three had been alive for thousands of years. They were old enough to make their own decisions. I hadn't forced them to fall for me. They had made that choice.

Time ticked by. The Reverend hadn't said what time it was when he came down, so I didn't know if another day was almost done. I just needed to do what he wanted for now, and then I would try to bolt again as soon as I could I told myself. Eventually he would get tired of me running and would either let me go, or kill me if I wasn't successful. I needed to try though. I had a whole life waiting for me out there that I had just discovered.

The light switched on. I drew a deep breath, preparing myself for whatever was going to come next. I could do this. The Reverend came down the stairs slowly. My resolve to play along weakened as he came into view. He was dressed in what I imagined was his version of groom's attire, a stiff black suit with a long, thick, red tie. I had always imagined my groom wearing a bowtie, but I guess since this wasn't my real wedding it would have to do. I really was losing it if that was a thought in my head.

Without speaking to me, he walked over and unlocked my cuff from the chain. He then took my arm firmly in his and walked me up the stairs, down the hallway, and into the room where I had stayed the first two nights. Laid out on the bed, looking freshly pressed, was what I assumed was my wedding gown. I instantly hated it.

"Put this on," he said sternly, pointing to the dress laying on the bed. "I will be coming to collect you soon. You will find everything you need to get ready in the bathroom."

After giving me one last look of warning, he walked out of the room. The lock clicked into place behind him.

Not wanting to examine the dress yet, I walked into the bathroom. Laid out neatly on the counter were a variety of cosmetics along with a brush. He hadn't left out anything remotely sharp that I could use as a weapon. Looking at the shower I debated whether to take one. He had made Anna stay in the room with me while I showered last time, not wanting to leave me alone for even a second. He didn't seem concerned about that now as he had left the room, but would he come in while I was showering?

I decided to risk it. A night in the woods followed by another stay in the basement meant that I was once again disgusting. I turned the shower on, threw off my clothes, and stepped in, surely breaking the record for the world's fastest shower with how fast I cleaned myself off. I stepped out and wrapped a towel around myself, walking over to the bed to examine the dress as I did so. There was a set of blood red, lacey underwear laying next to the dress that I hadn't noticed before. I shuddered, wondering if he had come in and left them there while I was showering.

Afraid that he would return soon, I slipped the undergarments on, knowing that red underwear would fill me with dread for the rest of my life. I stared down at the dress he wanted me to wear. I slowly stepped into it and zipped up the side zipper before turning to look at myself in the mirror that was in the room. It was fitted on top with a sweetheart neckline, before flouncing out with what felt like a hundred yards of tulle. There were little crystals all over the bodice. It looked like something someone would wear to prom I thought to myself idly. I wondered how he had managed to get something so close to my size.

Suddenly there was a knock on the door. I turned, nausea

turning my stomach as the Reverend opened the door. He turned, gaping at me, lust filling his expression.

"You look indescribable," he gasped at me. I again said nothing to him. If he was going to force me through this charade, I wasn't going to make it pleasant.

He took my arm and once again we went out into the hallway before walking into a large room I hadn't seen yet. There were at least fifteen to twenty bouquets of red roses placed around the room. The smell of roses permeated the air, turning my stomach. There was a large tv set up in the front of the room. The Reverend led me in front of the tv, reaching for a remote with the hand that wasn't holding mine.

The screen turned on, strangely showing a still shot of himself. The Reverend turned to me, his screen self also looking at me.

"I couldn't think of anyone better to bless this union than myself," he explained. "I recorded myself officiating our marriage earlier. Just answer as if another person was asking the questions."

I visibly blanched and this time he didn't ignore it.

"I gave you plenty of time to get used to this idea, Eva. Don't make this any harder than it needs to be," he scowled.

The recording began. The screen Reverend gave a spiel about how this union was blessed by the heavens. It then went on about the women's role, how the wife was meant to serve the husband, to make him happy at all costs. I couldn't believe what I was hearing.

The time came for us to exchange our vows. Despite my earlier pep talk to myself to go along with it, I couldn't find the strength to do it. Unbidden images came strolling through my mind of myself in a wedding gown, but this time one that I had chosen. I imagined Damon, Mason, and Beckham both in the place of the groom, separately, and then all together. This evil man didn't get to take my "I do" away from me.

The Reverend eagerly said yes when the screen him asked if he took me as his wife. The silence was deafening when it came time for me to speak. I stonily stared at him, my chin hard with determination. His face filled with rage as my time to speak passed, and the screen Reverend began to move on to the next portion of the recording.

"These vows will be binding before God no matter what you do," he said, spittle sprinkling my face from how hard he forced the words out in his anger. He smoothed out his face, taking a deep breath to calm down. We listened to the recording as it got to the part I was most dreading.

The screen Reverend droned "You may now kiss the bride."

The Reverend standing in front of me gave me a big smile, his eyes glittering with desire. He grabbed my chin and gave me a long, slimy kiss, his wormy tongue threatening to break into mine.

I pulled my head back from his grasp as hard as I could, gagging as I did so. The Reverend laughed in amusement and grabbed my hand, dragging me into the dining area where the Andersons had been murdered right before my eyes.

The table was laden with what looked like fine china. He pulled out a chair and forced me to sit in it. After sitting down he called out, "We are ready!" I held my breath as Anna came wobbling in. I couldn't help but gasp when I saw the state she was in. She looked like she had been beaten within an inch of her life. He had hacked off her hair and her face was barely recognizable with how bruised and broken it was.

I cried silent tears as she set food in front of us. She didn't look at me, and the guilt swarmed over me. This had happened to her because of me.

Anna left in between servings. I didn't touch my food of course, but the Reverend inhaled his food, going on and on about our new life together. The tingling in my back was getting worse as we sat there and my body began to feel like I was burning up from the inside. I wavered in my chair, feeling like I would pass out at any moment.

The Reverend finally finished his meal. Anna had disappeared again. He stood up from his chair and collected me, before marching me back down the hallway into my red and black bedroom. The same cloying scent of roses filled my nostrils as we walked in. There were red rose petals sprinkled all over the room. There was a single lamp in the corner. The glow from it made the room seem even more foreboding for some reason.

The door closed behind us, clicking as he locked it. This was it, I could see it in his eyes. I wasn't going to be able to put him off anymore. I turned to bolt, but he caught my arm, ripping off some of the tulle on the bottom of my dress with his exuberance when he stepped on it. Suddenly the tingling feeling that had been growing in intensity the last few days turned into more of a burn. I gasped in pain as my back felt like it was tearing in two. All of a sudden something popped out of me, tearing through the back of my dress.

The Reverend immediately let go of me, stepping back with wide, astonished eyes. I reached back with one hand, trying to see what was back there, while using my other hand to keep my ripped dress covering the front of myself. I yanked my hand back when I touched something that felt like feathers. Did I have freaking wings? Whatever they were, they felt like new appendages had sprouted from my body. They fluttered involuntarily, and I fell back a step at the sensation. The Reverend was still staring at me, his disbelief turning into wonder at whatever had sprang from my back.

He reached out a hand, his intent clear that he wanted to touch my "wings." I took a step back. My mind was spinning wondering if this had something to do with my birthday, and if any other special powers were going to make an appearance and save the day. I tried to take another step, but the new weight of the wings made it hard to keep my balance and I stumbled. I reached the door and pulled on it, forgetting for a second that the Reverend had somehow managed to lock it from this side. I was trapped.

Suddenly the room's temperature began to rapidly drop. I looked around wildly and sure enough, I saw the black shadow of a specter in the corner walking towards us. To my surprise, another specter appeared behind it, and then another. They continued to multiply until there were too many to count, filling the space around us.

The Reverend was looking around him. Lexi had told me that specters were invisible to normal humans, but that they could sense something was wrong when a specter was near them. The Reverend could definitely tell something was wrong.

He whirled around in a circle, trying to see what was in the room with us. All of a sudden the lamp was extinguished. Due to the heavy drapes on the windows, the room was almost as dark as the basement had been. I could hear the Reverend's breathing get faster as he began to panic.

"What are you doing?" he cried out, his voice quivering in fear.

"Nothing," I squeaked out, growing more fearful myself as I waited for the specters' icy touch.

"Evaaaaa..." called out an eerie voice from somewhere around us. It was impossible to tell where it was coming from, as it seemed to echo around the room. The Reverend was at this point huddled against me, pulling me in front of him as if I could protect him. My wings fluttered in fear as something brushed against them.

All of a sudden the Reverend was yanked away from me. He began to scream as the sound of ripping and something cracking filled the darkness around me.

I huddled against a wall. I was paralyzed with fear, not able to think clearly enough to try and get away. Not that I could go anywhere anyway with the locked door. The darkness of the room was stifling and all-encompassing. The heavy curtains over the windows made it impossible to even see my hand in front of my face, let alone whatever demon was in the room with me.

I heard the Reverend begging some unknown creature for mercy. A rush of hate flowed through me. Kylan Darcy did not deserve mercy. I immediately tried to push that thought away. I didn't need to feel that way.

The icy hand of a specter stroked down my face, almost as if it was trying to comfort me. I shuddered as the Reverend gave one last shriek before absolute silence filled the room.

The lamp flickered back on.

Kylan Darcy lay on the ground in a pool of blood. His face bloated into a look of horror. The fear I had been feeling increased tenfold. What creature had done this? And where was it now?

I suddenly heard breathing behind me. Whoever had done this was still in the room with me. Without any options of how to get away, I took a deep resolved breath and turned my head.

"Evaaaa," something called out in a sing song voice.

Strangely familiar piercing black eyes were my last view as a caustic powder enveloped my senses and the world faded.

Epilogue

I stood in front of him, trying to keep my spine straight, trying to remember why I was doing this. It was a soul shattering feeling to know I was on the precipice of taking this step, this colossal, ugly, eternity ending step.

Tears were sliding down Beckham's gorgeous face. I stared, lost in my own misery, as one drop dripped off his stubbled chin. If this were any other circumstance, I would have been horrified since I had never before seen him cry, not even when he was injured.

But I couldn't reach out to comfort him, even though I felt like I couldn't breathe, even though the need to take it all back was clawing up from inside of me desperate to save our love.

"Why are you doing this?" he whispered softly, his voice clogged up with sorrow.

I had gone back and forth over how I would do this. If I should deny I had ever felt anything, deny that we were a soul match so that maybe he would hate me and more easily move on. But I was selfish, I couldn't deny something that had meant everything to me since the moment that I met him. I would hide the memories of our time spent together, and the love that we *shared deep in my heart for when I needed it to get me through the long, never ending days ahead of me.*

"It is my duty as Queen," I answered. "I haven't been able to find any other way to save us." He dropped to his knees and buried his face in my stomach.

"I can't let you do this. I can't survive without you. Please choose me," he begged me.

I slowly slid to my knees and pressed my forehead against his. "This is not me not choosing you. This is me saving you. You will be in my heart until I draw my last breath. There will never be another for me but you."

The tears I had tried so hard to keep in streamed down my face, mingling with Beckham's until it was impossible to tell who the tears had fallen from. I was truly tempted in that moment, tempted to beg him to forgive me, and tell him I didn't mean anything I had said, when a cold voice called my name from the distance. My resolve came roaring back. I abruptly stood up, lovingly stroking a lock of Beckham's golden hair one last time before I turned away, leaving my past behind, and walking towards my future.

Continued in Forbidden Queens...

Author's Note

I've been literally blown away by the response to the first book of my little series. First Impressions reached the top of several lists on Amazon, I've been approached by publishers and literary agents, and I have gotten to hear from so many of you of how much you liked Eva's story. It truly means so much to hear from each of you. It makes all the long hours and stress so worth it to hear that it has touched even one of you.

I love Forgotten Specters. First Impressions was a little hard to write in that I knew I needed to lay a foundation for the series before I could really start Eva's journey. In Forgotten Specters, I felt like I was finally getting to start Eva's story. Book Three of the series, Forbidden Queens, is already in the works, as well as several novellas of the guys and other characters. I can't wait to continue to share Eva's world with you. It's only going to get more wild from here.

If you like it, please leave a review on Amazon to give me further motivation to keep the story going. As I've said before, reviews are the lifeblood of authors, and I read all of them.

Visit my **Facebook** page to get updates.

Visit my **Amazon Author** page.
Visit my **Website**.

Join my newsletter **here**. I post about new releases, give points of views that aren't in the books, and give you useless facts about myself.

About C.R. Jane

A Texas girl living in Utah now, I'm a wife, mother, lawyer, and now author. My stories have been floating around in my head for years, and it has been a relief to finally get them down on paper. I'm a huge Dallas Cowboys fan and I primarily listen to Taylor Swift and hip hop…don't lie and say you don't too.

My love of reading started probably when I was three and it only made sense that I would start to create my own worlds since I was always getting lost in others'.

I like heroines who have to grow in order to become badasses, happy endings, and swoon-worthy, devoted, (and hot) male characters. If this sounds like you, I'm pretty sure we'll be friends.

I'm so glad to have you on my team…check out the links below for ways to hang out with me and more of my books you can read!

Visit my **Facebook** page to get updates.

Visit my Website.

Sign up for my newsletter to stay updated on new releases,

find out random facts about me, and get access to different points of view from my characters.

Books by C.R. Jane

www.crjanebooks.com

The Sounds of Us Contemporary Series (complete series)

Remember Us This Way

Remember You This Way

Remember Me This Way

Broken Hearts Academy Series: A Bully Romance (complete duet)

Heartbreak Prince

Heartbreak Lover

Ruining Dahlia (Contemporary Mafia Standalone)

Ruining Dahlia

Pretty Madness (Omegaverse Standalone)

Pretty Madness

The Fated Wings Series (Paranormal series)

First Impressions

Forgotten Specters

The Fallen One (a Fated Wings Novella)

Forbidden Queens

Frightful Beginnings (a Fated Wings Short Story)

Faded Realms

Faithless Dreams

Fabled Kingdoms

Forever Hearts

The Rock God (a Fated Wings Novella)

The Darkest Curse Series

Forget Me

Lost Passions

Hades Redemption Series

The Darkest Lover

The Darkest Kingdom

Monster & Me Duet Co-write with Mila Young

Monster's Temptation

Monster's Obsession

Academy of Souls Co-write with Mila Young (complete series)

School of Broken Souls

School of Broken Hearts

School of Broken Dreams

School of Broken Wings

Fallen World Series Co-write with Mila Young (complete series)

Bound

Broken

Betrayed

Belong

Thief of Hearts Co-write with Mila Young (complete series)

Darkest Destiny

Stolen Destiny

Broken Destiny

Sweet Destiny

Kingdom of Wolves Co-write with Mila Young

Wild Moon

Wild Heart

Wild Girl

Wild Love

Wild Soul

Wild Kiss

Stupid Boys Series Co-write with Rebecca Royce

Stupid Boys

Dumb Girl

Crazy Love

Breathe Me Duet Co-write with Ivy Fox (complete)

Breathe Me

Breathe You

Breathe Me Duet

Rich Demons of Darkwood Series Co-write with May Dawson

Make Me Lie

Make Me Beg

Make Me Wild

Make Me Burn